Counterspy

Also by Matthew Dunn

SLINGSHOT
SENTINEL
SPYCATCHER

Coming Soon in Hardcover
DARK SPIES

Counterspy

A SPYCATCHER NOVELLA

MATTHEW DUNN

WILLIAM MORROW IMPULSE
An Imprint of HarperCollins*Publishers*

Excerpt from *Dark Spies* copyright © 2014 by Matthew Dunn.

EPub Edition AUGUST 2014 ISBN: 9780062309365

Print Edition ISBN: 9780062362216

10 9 8 7 6 5 4 3

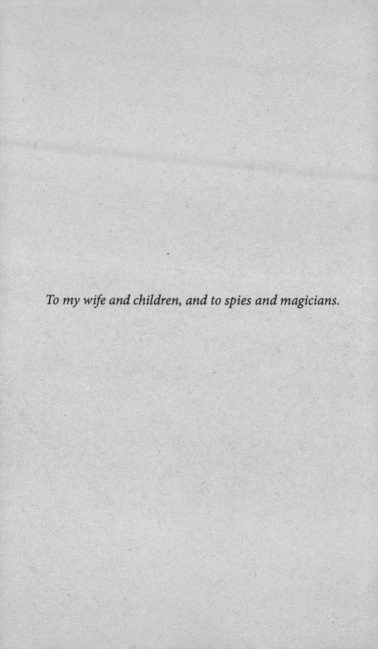

To my wife and children, and to spies and magicians.

Chapter 1

BEING DROWNED WAS not part of the deal, but the victim put up with it because so much was at stake.

And even though drowning sucked, the victim had survived it before, when he was five years old and couldn't stay afloat in the deep end of his parents' ornate swimming pool in their palatial Rajasthan residence. Then his distraught mother had yanked him out of the pool and summoned a kind Sikh doctor, who'd held him upside down to get the water out of his lungs.

Now, age twenty-two, the diminutive Indian was being pinned down by four CIA men who were the antithesis of the Sikh doctor. They were in a bare cell in a top-secret U.S. military base in Afghanistan, and the CIA men were using a towel and a bucket to put water in his lungs and make his body convulse in agony. They called it waterboarding.

It sounded like a kind of sport the Indian's rich friends played on the shores of Goa.

But there was nothing sporting about this. It was torture of the very worst kind—just one splash of water onto the towel convinced you you were going to die. Most people broke at this point, and that's why the Agency used the technique. But today the CIA officers were cursing, shouting, and red faced with impatience because the victim was being drowned for the fourth time and showed no signs of breaking.

Their anger was exacerbated by the fact that the Indian hadn't uttered a word to his captors in the two days since they'd grabbed him in a remote farm in Kapisa province, put a hood over his head and shackles on his sinewy arms and legs, thrown him into the back of a jeep, and driven fast over ground that had been rough enough to toss the man's body up and down. Since that agonizing journey, the victim had been kept in isolation on the base, stripped naked, blasted with a power hose, slapped around the face, struck in the gut with socks filled with wet sand, and forced into agonizing stress positions.

Throughout his brief but excruciating period of incarceration, the only people he'd seen were the four men. He didn't know their names; all they'd told him about themselves was that they answered to no one aside from the head of the CIA, the president of the United States, and God. The Indian thought that the introduction had been somewhat presumptuous, because when he was ten his Muslim father had given him a copy of the Bible and told him to read it cover to cover so that he could understand that Christianity wasn't a bad religion. As far as he could recall, there was no reference in the Bible to CIA officers being authorized agents of God.

And right now he wasn't sure his father was right, because the four men didn't seem like good people. On the contrary, they looked like the bad guys he'd seen in the old Hollywood movies his wealthy father had projected onto a huge screen so that the poor kids in their local village could get ninety minutes of escapism. Wearing matching white shirts, sleeves rolled up, suit trousers, and smart wingtips, the CIA men could have been gangsters, corrupt detectives, or contract killers.

When the men had raced into his home while he'd been kneeling toward Mecca and asking Allah for forgiveness, they'd smashed his face against his prayer mat. He'd had no doubt that it wouldn't be the last act of violence inflicted on him by the officers. But he'd known that he had to stay strong if he was to survive, so he'd tried to pretend the bad things that had been happening to him had not been real, and instead he was in a 1950s movie that would end very soon.

To help him perpetuate the mind trick, he'd secretly ascribed each CIA officer a name.

Jack Palance, Lee Marvin, Henry Fonda, Robert Mitchum.

Their eyes held hate, and they swaggered with the physicality of men whose bodies were naturally chiseled and tough and didn't need to spend one minute in a gym. They were bruisers who could tear someone twice their size into pieces.

And yet the Indian was half their size but physically and mentally far superior to the CIA officers. They were huffing and puffing, and all the while they didn't know that they were in a movie of the victim's choosing and that he was waiting for the moment when he could say something of vital importance. A moment when they thought he was a broken and truthful man.

That would happen after the fifth drowning, the victim had decided at the commencement of the waterboarding.

At that point, the four heavies would believe anything that came out of his waterlogged mouth.

Palance grabbed the Indian's hair, pulled his head to within inches of his V-shaped jaw, and used the same menacing tone. "We hate you."

Mitchum toweled the sweat off his arms and face and shoved the stinking rag back over the victim's face.

Fonda leaned in close, his piercing blue eyes identical to those of the psychopathic gunman in *Once Upon a Time in the West.* "We know you understand English because of all the English books we found at your home. So listen to me carefully. We'll keep waterboarding you until you die."

Marvin nodded at his colleagues, took a swig from a liter bottle of mineral water whose label proclaimed WATER GIVES LIFE, spat the mouthful onto the Indian's face, and poured the remaining contents onto the rag. Marvin's spit and the water went the wrong way down the victim's gullet and made him think he was back in his family's swimming pool; head throbbing, limbs thrashing, lungs in agony.

Mitchum let out a loud belch and laughed before asking, "Who are you?"

When the rag was removed and the Indian stopped

gagging, he decided that Mitchum's question was the only reasonable one he'd heard since being imprisoned.

Because he wasn't a victim at all. He was a man whose base of operations in Kapisa had guns, bomb-making equipment, and numerous cell phones containing the numbers of known terrorists. After someone had tipped off the Agency, he'd been caught red-handed with the equipment by men who knew what he was but didn't know his name.

Mitchum waved the dripping rag in front of the Indian's face. He no longer looked angry and held an expression that momentarily perplexed the Indian. Mitchum sighed, glanced at his colleagues, and returned his attention to the captive. "This is your choice, not ours. Best we get this over with."

Of course—Mitchum's expression was one that some men have when they realize that every other option had been fruitlessly pursued and all that was left was death.

The Indian could not and would not let that happen. He shook his head, hoping he looked petrified even though in truth he felt calm and very much in control.

It was the same feeling he'd always had as a teenager when amazing his fellow students and teachers by performing acts of escapology on the stage at his boarding school. Padlocked metal boxes, water tanks, chains and ropes lashed around him—he'd escaped them all and had never once felt fear or doubt that he would succeed. Now was no different, although he had to look and sound like a wretched and terrified victim in order to be convincing. "Please . . . please, I beg you to stop."

"Begging's of no use to you." Fonda pointed at him. "All it does is prove to us that you're weak scum."

The Indian wished he could tell the American that his observation was wholly inaccurate, because after the swimming pool accident he'd spent the rest of his life honing his physical and mental skills so that he would never be weak again. "I . . . I will tell you anything you need to know. But please, please, no more water."

Palance yanked the Indian's arm to sit him upright. "That's more like it. Talking's good. We need your name, who you work for, and details of your targets."

The Indian lowered his head.

"Head up!"

He did as he was told, looking at the other men before returning his attention to Palance. This was the moment he'd been waiting for, the time for the words that he'd been reciting in his head ever since he'd been imprisoned. "I'm an Indian intelligence officer, code name Trapper. My role in Afghanistan has been to operate deep cover to infiltrate terrorist cells."

All of the men frowned.

"Indian intelligence?" Mitchum looked unsettled. "Research and Analysis Wing?"

The R&AW was India's primary external intelligence agency.

Trapper nodded. "My cover's been intact for three years since I've been in the country. Now I'm not so sure. Who sold me out to you?"

Fonda answered, "We got ourselves a source. Says you're a bomber, among other things."

"A source?"

"Yeah, but you ain't getting his name." Mitchum looked at the rag he was holding. "If what you're saying is true, it sounds like your cover's still intact. People still think you're a terrorist. But I'm thinking you could be spinning us a crock of bullshit. We're going to need to check you out with R&AW."

Trapper had anticipated this and responded carefully. "Only R&AW senior management is cleared to know my code name and what I'm doing here. They're going to be very pissed you grabbed me. You could call them. But if I were you, I'd send someone in person to smooth waters."

Marvin leaned closer to Trapper's face. "That could take hours to arrange, maybe days."

"I'm prepared to wait; I urge you to do the same."

The room was silent. The four men were clearly thinking through options.

Fonda broke the silence. "Alright." He pointed at the bottle of water. "No more of this stuff while we get your story checked out." He said to his colleagues, "Put him back in his cell."

When the Indian was on his feet, he said in an imploring tone, "Would whoever you send to R&AW headquarters please be kind enough to relay to my bosses that I didn't break cover until the fifth waterboarding?"

Fonda nodded. "I've not seen anyone hold out this long. I respect that. We'll make sure your management knows you kept your mouth shut longer than we thought possible."

"Thank you."

By the time his captors had received confirmation from R&AW that Trapper's claim was a complete lie, Trapper would have escaped his cell and vanished.

"There's one more thing." Trapper looked directly at Fonda, deciding that he was the highest-ranking officer in the room. "I know from one of my terrorist affiliates that a senior CIA officer is being targeted for assassination. It's revenge for the officer's assassination of a high-ranking Taliban leader. I was about to relay that to R&AW so that they could pass on the intelligence to you guys, but then," he shrugged, "you guys stormed my house and brought me here."

Fonda, Palance, Mitchum, and Marvin stared at him.

Fonda asked, "Does the CIA officer have a name?"

Trapper rubbed water off his face, hair, and chest while wondering if the Agency torturers would grab him for doing so without their permission. Instead, they were motionless and expectant. Just as he'd imagined they would be when, weeks ago, he'd constructed his plan to get to this moment, had made an anonymous call to the Agency's headquarters in Langley, and had given the secret location of an Indian Muslim terrorist who was hiding in Afghanistan and who happened to be him. Nearly everything the Agency operatives in the room thought was real was in fact an almighty sleight of hand. But two things were not false: the very real threat to the CIA officer and his name.

Trapper was motionless in the center of the room, water still dripping off his thin but strong body. He imagined his captors' surprise when they realized he'd escaped from his cell using a penknife he'd stolen from Mitchum's pocket while the agent had been pouring water down his throat. "His name is Will Cochrane."

Chapter 2

MY EARLIEST MEMORY of feeling gut-wrenchingly scared
was on a sweaty Virginia day when a rotund nag of a
lady, who we called Eat Less, locked her puffy eyes on
the other kids in my class before pointing at me. "Will
Cochrane," she said with the solemnity of an executioner,
"I have absolutely no doubt that you will fail in adult-
hood just as much as you're failing in school." The other
children sniggered as they looked at me; my face flushed
red with embarrassment. But worse was the feeling in my
gut: a cascade of demented pulsations that had made me
think I should run to the school nurse and tell her to stop
making me a failure. Two years before, age five, I'd made
the decision to be man of the house because my American dad had been captured and subsequently killed while
working for the CIA in the Middle East, and my English
mom and sister needed me. Being a failure was therefore
not an option.

But I couldn't run, because Eat Less waddled across the room with speed that didn't look fast but was—a bit like a running hippopotamus. She grabbed my thin arm and put her pimply nose against mine, an act that coupled my fear with revulsion, and repeated, "Failure, failure, failure." Later, I gained solace when my mom explained that this was deemed inappropriate and Eat Less had been sacked. But in the classroom at the time I was a quivering wreck because I was a flop and apparently always would be.

I felt another kind of fear, but no less intense, as I walked through a subterranean tunnel in Washington, D.C., pistol in hand, sewage up to my calves; rats, shit, and piss everywhere. A man, somewhere ahead, would happily gut me with his knife before using it to gouge out my eyes and slice off my head.

People who knew my background could be forgiven for thinking that abject fear was anathema to a person like me. I was, on paper at least, not only an example of why Mrs. Eat Less's prophecies were wholly inaccurate but also living testament to the fact that teenagers who play viola in their school orchestra are not necessarily going to grow up to be pushovers, contrary to what the high school jocks believed when they kicked in my head and called me a faggot.

When I was seventeen, I knifed to death four criminals who'd killed my mother and were about to do the same to my sister. The next day, I fled to France and spent five battered and bruising years in the French Foreign Legion. After completing my tour with the Legion, I studied at Cambridge University and gained a first class honors degree before catching the attention of MI6, who recruited and trained me. For the last nine years, MI6 deployed me as a top-secret joint MI6-CIA operative combating the very worst of the world's secret ills. One might deduce that all of that experience should have numbed my nerve endings, much like the nerves that die beneath a scab that is picked over and over again.

But I needed my nerves to stay sharp, because without them I couldn't achieve anything, much less any sense of happiness. The trade-off, however, was that attuned nerves begot other emotions, such as loneliness, sorrow, and fear.

So be it, I thought as I walked though near darkness that was only alleviated by occasional wall lights. This was what I'd been trained for. This was what I do, time and time again. Kill bad guys, steal secrets, stop genocide, protect the West, go places other men refuse to go.

But men, or at least their excrement, had gotten here before me; plus, somewhere ahead, was a Russian guy called Abram, who—among many achievements in his life—had covertly fought in the Bosnian conflict as a Russian special forces operative, earned millions extracting blood diamonds from Africa and selling them to line the pocket of the Russian premier, sung "Nessun dorma!" pitch perfect at a Carnegie Hall Russian-American charity gala, volunteered his services to me because he believed Russian foreign policy was as likely to bring world peace as the Eurovision Song Contest, and turned out to be a lying, duplicitous bastard who'd tried to murder me nine minutes ago on a day that signified I'd been on earth for exactly thirty-five years.

The attempt had happened in a nice Italian restaurant four blocks from here; one where red wine was served in carafes and the atmosphere was full of the sound of opera, laughter, and the aroma of garlic.

Abram and I had been sitting opposite each other, eating a starter of barley mushroom risotto while discussing the recent reshuffle within the Kremlin. The meal had been going well, but then Abram—maybe mimicking young Michael Corleone in *The Godfather*—had pulled out a gun and tried to shoot me in the head. It had been wrong on many levels, not least because I'd been really hungry and looking forward to a main course of meatballs enriched with lemon peel.

I'd swiped the gun away from his hand; he'd slapped me in the face, then the throat. All perfect moves, though under the circumstances it must have looked to other diners like we'd been a gay couple who'd finally had enough of each other. Abram had turned and bolted out of the restaurant while withdrawing a knife; I'd upended the table, pulled out my gun, and pursued. This was, the witnesses must have thought, a tiff that had turned really nasty.

Chasing Abram was problematic, because he was clever and swift. I'd screamed at people to get down while I'd run through the rain-sodden metropolitan night and tried to get a line of sight on him. His use of D.C.'s sewage systems was obviously a preplanned escape route should things go wrong, and it was only because I'd been running fast that I'd managed to catch a glimpse of him disappearing under a manhole cover, like a rabid polecat entering a rabbit warren.

I'd always known that Abram's nasty. In my line of work I'd mixed with people like that a lot, and in fairness to Abram he's not the worst person I'd partnered with to attempt to screw the East in favor of satiating the West. Until this evening, I'd ranked Abram as a seven out of ten bad guy. But Abram's stock had just gone up, and as I waded through crap I tried to decide whether he was an eight, nine, or ten out of ten.

Maybe these were superfluous thoughts, because a man who will slit your throat is a man who will slit your throat, and his ranking won't make the experience better or worse. But I thought about it anyway, as it helped me ignore the heat within the labyrinth of tunnels and the noise in my ears from the drumbeat of my heart.

Part of me hoped Abram would keep running and use his knowledge of one of the oldest sewage systems in the States to his advantage. I knew nothing about the maze I was in, and every step I took furthered the possibility that I wouldn't be able to find my way out of here. Trouble was, getting out of the sewer was the least of my problems, because Abram wanted me dead and I couldn't think of a more perfect venue in which he could enact his crime.

I reached a junction in the tunnel where I needed to make a decision to turn left or right. Standing still, I listened, trying to ignore the thump of my heartbeat, the rank odor, and the scurrying and splashing of vermin.

A louder noise came from my left; whoosh, whoosh, whoosh; maybe a man kicking his leg through ankle-deep water. That made sense, because Abram didn't want me to make the wrong turn. He needed me to hear and follow him until I reached a place of his choosing so he could surprise me.

I made no attempt to be quiet as I moved down a tunnel that was narrower than the previous one and clearly wasn't flushed as frequently, because the smell was making me gag. My handgun at eye level, I waded onward, imagining my MI6 controller declaring to the chief of British Intelligence, "Will Cochrane died in shit."

I didn't want to die in shit. I didn't want to die at all. I had things to do, such as mastering the Chaconne Baroque lute recital, completing my thesis on loose-leaf Chinese teas, going to the river Itchen for the first time and casting a fly line, and trying to find a woman who'd have me. These and other things were important, and it pissed me off that multiple times each year I found myself in situations where I'd put all of my aspirations in jeopardy.

The wall lights—bare bulbs that were throwing off a dull, yellow glow—were fewer now, some flickering. Large chunks of the tunnel were in complete darkness. Most likely, Abram had concealed himself in the shadows, waiting to attack. Although he was twelve years older than me and had left the military over a decade ago, he was fit and strong, and in his spare time he kept up the crazy Russian special forces tests to try to be immune to pain. As I moved into one of the chunks of darkness,

I decided that if he managed to disarm me, I wasn't sure which of us would better the other.

The slash of Abram's knife across my forearm, which made me drop my pistol, meant I was about to find out.

Instinctively, I twisted my body a split second before I saw the tiniest glint of steel thrust into the space where I'd been standing. I grabbed his knife-wielding arm and twisted it hard. He punched his knee into my ribs. But I kept the lock on despite the agony in my body, yanked back his wrist, saw the knife drop out of his hand, twisted his arm further so that he was completely off balance, and dragged him with me so that he had no choice but to fall to the ground. I maintained my grip on his limb as I placed my foot on his throat and forced his head underwater.

I had to use all of my strength to hold him there; his legs were thrashing and his free arm was punching my foot and trying to wrench it free from his throat. It felt like ten minutes but was actually nearer two when Abram stopped moving. I kept his head under for another minute in case he was trying to trick me into releasing my hold on him. But after that, I reached down and pulled his head out.

No doubt about it; he was dead.

Chapter 3

OFFICIALLY THERE ARE eight directors who report to the head of the Central Intelligence Agency. Although most of them are not publicly named, their job title and rank are available for all to see on the Agency's website. But I knew a secret that's only privy to a handful of senior CIA officers, the president of the U.S., my London-based MI6 controller, and the prime minister of Britain: there's a ninth director in the Agency. His name's Patrick, and he and my MI6 controller head up the joint task force that I work for. Barely anyone in Western intelligence knows about it.

I was standing in an empty room within the Agency's headquarters in Langley, and I was facing Patrick. He's a tall, sinewy, ex-army officer type, twenty years my senior, and was normally immaculately dressed, his expression composed. But today I was somewhat perturbed to see that he had his shirtsleeves rolled up and his rattlesnake face on—a term I use when his eyes go mean.

I had hoped today would be routine: filling in paperwork, telling the truth about Abram's assault on me in the restaurant, lying that he'd escaped, and not telling the truth that I'd left his body to the rats. After all, it was only a few hours ago that I'd managed to find a way out of the sewer and had caused everyone in the lobby of the Mandarin Oriental hotel to stare at me with mouths wide open as I'd walked toward the elevators while covered in crap. And even when I'd gotten to my room, it had taken three showers and two baths before I'd been satisfied that I was clean enough to hit the sack. I was tired and needed today to be a boring one.

But here was Patrick. With that look.

"What's up, old boy?" I asked in my best hammed-up British accent, fully cognizant it would severely antagonize the rattlesnake.

"Aside from the fact that your presence in D.C. was supposed to be discreet—no assassination attempts on you, no guns drawn, zero civilians screaming as they see you running through the streets, pretty much nothing out of the ordinary until you get on a plane and head back to the UK?"

"Aside from that fact, yes." I smiled insincerely. It always made Patrick want to punch my face. "Anyway, you can't blame me because people want to kill me."

"I can. The fact that people want to kill you means that they are troubled by your character or actions. And that means you have social problems that are wholly your responsibility."

I thought Patrick had a point. "I did nothing wrong."

"Running in a public place with a pistol in your hand? You were lucky you weren't shot by a cop."

Simply for the sake of seeing what it would do to Patrick, I wanted to tell him that it got much worse than that, but I decided that confessing I'd killed Abram on U.S. soil wouldn't work in my favor. "Something else is bothering you."

Patrick looked at me in a way that always made me feel that he was my surrogate father or uncle. The look killed my flippant posturing.

And rightly so. He was my father's colleague, secretly gave financial support to my mother after my dad was killed, and had consistently backed me to the hilt even though privately he sometimes told me I was a frickin' damn liability.

Patrick kept his eyes focused on mine. "You know why Abram tried to take a shot at you?"

I nodded. "Russia's wanted me dead for years. Turns out Abram's been loyal to the Russians all along. They used him to get to me."

Patrick tapped his hand on a telephone. "Yeah, well, we've spoken to the Kremlin. Told 'em that one of our own was targeted by one of theirs and that if anything similar happens again we'll post on the Internet a video we got of a certain senior Russian politician having a good time with a woman who's not his wife. That should keep Russia off your back for a while."

"Great."

"No, it's not all great, because it's possible Russia's not the only one that wants you dead."

He told me about a man, code name Trapper, who was seized by Agency men in Afghanistan, lied that he was an Indian intelligence officer, said that I was being targeted for execution by unknown terrorists because I'd killed a senior Taliban leader, and escaped from a cell that was deemed to be totally escape-proof.

"Trapper's vanished," Patrick said. "I can understand why he fed them the intelligence officer shit; bought him time to escape. But I don't get why he went out of his way to say you were being targeted. Nor do I know how he got your name. You think there could be any truth in what he's said?"

"In principle, yes. I've lost count of the number of terrorists I've killed, including Taliban."

Patrick smiled, and this worried me. "I got to take precautions. Keep you here until we find Trapper and sort this out."

"For how long?" I had a sinking feeling.

"As long as it takes."

The prospect of having to kill days, maybe weeks, sitting in my hotel room was the last thing I wanted. I liked my hotel, but I'm a restless type, and sustained boredom makes me prone to grumpiness and moments of unexplained whimsy. The last time I had nothing to do was a three-week stint in a hotel in Vienna. By the end of that stint, I'd bought two awful paintings and a coat that hadn't suited me but most certainly would have looked good on Liberace, and nearly thrown my room's TV out the window because it had shown only one English-language movie and I'd watched it seven times. To this day, I still knew every line in *Finding Nemo.* "Let me go after Trapper."

"Can't afford for you to be taken out by a bunch of bearded crazies. There are some other big projects looming that we need you for."

"I'll find Trapper quicker than anyone else, plus I can handle myself against crazies."

Patrick adopted his cross daddy look. "I'm not taking that risk."

I could see Patrick's mind was made up. "I'll go mad in my hotel."

"I know. So, I'm thinking we move you to an Agency safe house. Get you off the radar. The place has got a housekeeper, so she'll be there to feed you and keep you company."

This was very bad news. There are two categories of CIA safe house keepers: the mothering type who spends every waking hour trying to make you fat; or the haughty type who thinks the house belongs to her and must remain spotless. Both types are always over sixty. "When do I move in?"

"Today."

FIVE HOURS LATER I exited a taxi in a quiet residential suburb, grabbed my bag, paid the driver, then considered asking him to take me back to central D.C. because the place around me looked like it could be in the top league of the world's most boring locations. On either side of the street the houses were identical and had manicured front lawns. I discerned no sign of life, meaning everyone was away at work or the occupants of the street were in their eighties and spent all day watching TV. It would have been better if the Agency had housed me in a downtrodden crime zone, because at least then there might have been something interesting going on around me.

But I let the taxi go and walked toward the safe house while deciding that if its keeper was the haughty type, I would make an extra effort to be as messy as possible, and if she was the mothering type, I would lie to her that I'm gluten and lactose intolerant. I knocked on the door, it opened, and I was very surprised to see that the person standing in front of me was a superb CIA field operative.

Her name, one of many but it's the one I like the most, was Chrissie Lime. Though I hadn't dared to ask her for her age, I guessed she was about five years younger than me, but despite her comparative youth she had eight years of operational work under her belt plus a degree from Harvard.

"Hi, Chrissie, are you still single?" I wondered why I blurted this question without thinking.

She pretended to look annoyed and responded in her New England accent, "Yes."

"That's a shame."

"You mean that?"

"Not sure. I guess it's a matter of perspective." From my perspective I was glad she wasn't hitched, because I had to admit I'd felt a bit of a feeling in my gut when I'd first laid eyes on her two years ago in Hanoi. She'd been operating under diplomatic cover in the U.S. embassy in Vietnam, recruiting spies and sending them over the border into southern China. I'd been visiting the country with the primary remit to do a review for a nonexistent holiday magazine, with the secondary remit to place a bomb under a car that was owned by a slave trader of children. Chrissie had been my in-country point of contact and the person who would supply me with the equipment I'd need for the job. After I'd turned the trader into a charred corpse, I'd invited Chrissie out for a drink at the Bamboo Bar in the Sofitel Metropole. It had been the unprofessional thing to do because we were supposed to have been keeping our contact to a minimum, but, like mischievous kids, spies sometimes cannot resist doing things that fly in the face of their tradecraft training. I'd sat in the bar, my beer encapsulated by hands that had still smelled of cordite; she'd walked in—tall, slender, black trouser suit, white shirt, shades, dark hair pinned up—and moved across the room with the confidence, charisma, and beauty of a movie star who was about to address a pack of photojournalists. She'd sat next to me, ordered a whiskey, looked me in the eye, and said, "You're not going to screw me tonight."

I'd respected that, and in any case it hadn't been my intention to tempt her into my bed, though the moment she'd told me that option had been off the table I'd felt a twang of disappointment but also a sense of optimism, because the word *tonight* was time-specific, meaning there was always the possibility of another day. We'd had quite a lot of drinks, and she'd made me laugh by telling me about the time she'd posed as a white Kenyan arms dealer while meeting an Iranian defense attaché in a restaurant in Switzerland that had overlooked the Alps and, for some reason unbeknownst to her, had bizarrely and wholly inaccurately said to him that the vista around them had reminded her of Kenya. I'd made her laugh by recalling the time I'd spent one year making preparations to lure a rogue nuclear physicist to a meeting with me, travelled to Nicosia to have dinner with him in my hotel's restaurant, had twenty minutes to spare after dressing in my room, put the TV on, and become so engrossed in a live AC/DC rock concert that I'd lost track of time and missed the meeting.

After that evening in Hanoi, Chrissie had been posted somewhere else, I'd been whisked off to do more covert operations, and our paths had never crossed again until this moment.

She was dressed like she was when I last saw her, and physically identical; I was getting the same feeling in my gut.

"Can I come in?" I felt like a sheepish boyfriend who was trying to get his girl back after an argument.

Chrissie didn't answer; instead she went into the living room, sat on a sofa, and examined me. "Since we last met, you've lost seven pounds, have nine more visible scars, and look like you've recently killed someone."

"How can you tell?"

"Which bit?"

"The killing bit."

She pointed at my face. "When I met you before you killed the target in Hanoi, your eyes were clear; after, they were dead. You've got the latter look right now."

"Actually, I think I'm just tired."

She clicked her tongue but didn't articulate that she knew I was lying.

"Why are you here?"

Chrissie rested an ankle on her leg and cracked her knuckles. "I was at a loose end in Langley—not due back in the field for another month—and Patrick thought I was the ideal candidate to keep an eye on you."

"I don't need watching."

"Patrick disagrees. Thinks that you wouldn't last one day with one of the normal safe house keepers; that you'd walk out the back door when she wasn't looking and just keep walking."

I feigned annoyance. "He's probably right." A thought occurred to me. "Maybe Patrick's decided it's time for me to settle down and get myself a good wife. He's thrown us together to see how things work out."

Chrissie raised her eyebrows while pointing at the ceiling. "My room's upstairs. It's got a lock on the door." She nodded toward the hallway. "You're on the first floor."

I sighed. "So what happens now?"

Chrissie jumped to her feet. "We need food, booze, and some good rental movies, so let's go shopping."

Two minutes later I was about to enter Chrissie's car, when my cell rang. The number was withheld, but I knew it was Langley because no one else had my number. I smiled as I answered because I was really pleased to be going shopping with a woman, which hadn't happened to me for a long time, and especially so because the woman was Chrissie. I answered the call. "Yeah?"

I could hear breathing at the end of the line, before a man who was definitely not Patrick said, "Mr. Cochrane, this is Trapper." His English was flawless, no hint of an accent. I'd never heard his voice before. "I'm calling out of courtesy to let you know that I've arrived in the United States of America. It's imperative that we meet soon, because I need to kill you."

Chapter 4

I GOT OUT of bed, having barely slept during the night. The evening before, Chrissie had been great company. We'd cooked together, eschewed her movie choice of a costume drama and mine of a real-life Navy SEAL mission in favor of Scrabble, which she'd emphatically won, drunk wine, and, at one point, engaged in the briefest of eye contact, which I'd interpreted as meaningful but probably hadn't been—at least, not on her part.

Chrissie had been making an effort to distract me. Patrick had told her about Trapper and what he'd said in Afghanistan, and I'd told her about yesterday's call from Trapper because she deserved to know she was cohabiting with a man who was being hunted. For a few hours, Chrissie had done a good job, but after I'd taken myself to bed, thoughts had raced through my mind throughout the night. The most dominant of them all was that I hated being taunted by a killer while I was in hiding. But it seemed that Patrick had bigger plans for me, so I was temporarily on the shelf with my hands tied behind my back.

But at least there was comfort that Chrissie was here.

I wasn't concerned about her being near me, because CIA safe houses are given that name for a reason. They're anonymous, secret, and sold every six months so that new houses can be purchased. No one outside of Langley knows their locations, and even within the Agency, that knowledge is limited to a handful of people. But I was concerned that the more time I spent with Chrissie, the greater the likelihood that I would make a pass at her and she would rebut me.

At one point during my restless night, I'd attempted to think about other things by recalling my evening with Chrissie in Vietnam and how we'd amicably bickered yesterday evening about whether our Szechuan chicken dish should contain one or two fresh chilies. At approximately 2:00 a.m., while fruitlessly trying to sleep, I'd decided I'd like to marry Chrissie.

Now, in the cold light of day, it seemed the silly thought of an inactive man prone to boredom.

No, I thought as I showered and dressed, this was not one of my capricious moments. It felt more real. Impetuous and gushing, yes. But real.

I walked out of the room, heard sizzling noises, and smelled bacon and sausages. Chrissie was in the kitchen, wearing a sharp suit, nudging food in a frying pan. It seemed she was cooking for the both of us. I was surprised, because I had her down as a wheatgrass-smoothie-on-the-go-breakfast girl. Many things about

Chrissie were surprising me. It all made me wonder if I should buy her a diamond ring today.

I needed a coffee and probably a slap in the face to snap out of it.

Instead those imperatives were curtailed by a call to my secret phone.

Trapper said, "I think you're in Washington, D.C.," and hung up.

I rang the number back but knew he wouldn't answer because it was a landline, almost certainly a public pay phone. I muttered, "Shit," and saw that Chrissie was looking at me.

"Him?"

I nodded. "Him."

She flipped bacon. "How's he got your number?"

"No idea."

"You going to tell Patrick?"

"That would be the sensible course of action."

"And yet, why's Trapper taunting you?"

"Precisely."

She tossed me her spatula, winked, and said, "Your turn to play housewife."

I complied, placed Chrissie's food on a plate, and ensured my bacon was singed to the point of being black, because I like meat but not if it resembles meat—the result, I guess, of seeing the remains of human flesh too many times. "You know what I'm thinking?"

Chrissie leaned against a bench, her arms folded. I thought she might be checking me out, but I wasn't sure. "Yes."

"And you're going to tell me I'm an idiot?"

"I should."

"But you're not going to?"

Chrissie stood next to me, looked in the pan, and said, "You're burning your bacon." She placed her hand on mine; it was the nicest thing that had happened to me in a long time. "If you tell Patrick that Trapper's in the States and is in contact with you, he'll task an Agency team to go after Trapper. Trapper will go to ground, and he'll keep doing so until he gets you on your own."

Chrissie was right, which was why I knew I'd no choice but to leave the safe house and go after Trapper. "You'll cover for me?"

Chrissie nodded. "If Patrick calls, I'll tell him you're a pain in the ass to be around, but otherwise you're doing as you're told—watching TV, reading books, doing nothing remotely interesting."

After breakfast, I packed my bag and called a cab. When it arrived, I was standing in the hallway, ready to go. Chrissie was with me, silent. I breathed in deeply, summoned up every ounce of courage I had, and asked, "When I'm finished, can I take you out to dinner somewhere nice?"

I fully expected her to say no.

Instead, she approached me, brushed a finger against my face, briefly kissed me on my cheek, looked at me in a way that was undeniably meaningful, and whispered, "Yes."

I was in heaven.

Two minutes and thirty-nine seconds later, as my cab

pulled away from the safe house, that feeling vanished, because Trapper called again and said, "We must meet tomorrow. Alone. I will call tomorrow at ten p.m. with precise instructions. If you bring anyone with you, I will kill them just before I kill you."

Chapter 5

THE REAL NAME of the Indian man who called himself
Trapper was Sahir.

It means "magician."

Sahir had often wondered how his parents could have
known that their newborn son would develop into someone who would excel in trickery. Perhaps they hadn't
known and it was mere luck that his name had matched
his subsequent hobby, or maybe he'd unwittingly de-
veloped his talents to give meaning to his identity. He'd
never asked his parents for their opinion on this, and
now he'd never know, because his father had been shot
in the head, and his grief-stricken mother had thrown
herself off a sheer face of the Guru Shikhar mountain.

That had happened one year ago, and it had left Sahir
alone in the world. He had no siblings, and his extended
family had turned their backs on him in disgust after his
parents had decided that their wealth should be inherited

by their only son. But being alone had never bothered Sahir because he liked being the gray man; the person who could move unnoticed amid throngs of people and do things that they would least expect.

Now was going to be one of those times, for the benefit of his amusement and the nearby homeless amputee war veteran who was lying on a sidewalk, fruitlessly begging for a few dollars.

Sahir was sitting at a table in an alfresco D.C. café, wearing a silk shirt, expensive slacks, and shoes, sipping black tea, and enjoying the early morning sunshine wash over his smooth skin. He fit in here because every table around him was occupied by other rich people who looked good on the outside, though they didn't appear to share Sahir's inner sense of calm. To him, they seemed brash, angry with life, and they spoke only in negatives. As a child, Sahir had heard about the American Dream and had marveled at the notion that an entire nation could have a collective notion of happiness. It had made him envious and confused, because in India there are so many different visions of success. But now that he was in the States, he decided that if the American Dream was true, the people around him hadn't experienced it yet.

One tall and well-groomed man, three tables away from Sahir, seemed particularly affronted with life. He was talking loudly to four friends, all of whom—like him—were wearing thousand-dollar suits and watches that would have cost ten times that much. He was using racist language to declare that D.C. was going to shit because liberal jerks on Capitol Hill wanted all American cities to turn into faggoty, tree-hugging social experiments.

Sahir decided that the man was a pernicious idiot savant, because he was clearly gifted at garnering wealth but had a mental blind spot when it came to the joy that can be derived from being compassionate. That meant Sahir had to punish him.

Sahir finished his tea, left a tip on the table for the waiter, and moved to the angry man, who was now jabbing his finger on the table in time with each embittered word he spoke.

"Sir, I would like to perform a trick and was wondering if you'd participate?"

The man looked flummoxed. "A trick?" He glanced at his friends before returning his gaze to the Indian. "You're joking me, right?"

Sahir smiled in a confident yet respectful way. "I am an amateur magician." He waved his hand in a flourish. "I need a participant and an audience to practice my craft."

One of the man's female friends giggled and said, "Go on, Carl. Sounds fun."

No doubt Carl didn't agree. "You live here?"

"No, sir. I'm visiting your country, and when I've finished doing so, I will return to my country and will never bother you again."

The woman was now laughing and said, "Come on, Carl, he's obviously not one of *them* guys you're talking about. Give it a go."

Carl looked cornered. "What do I have to do?"

Sahir smiled wider. "Simply stand in front of me and extend your hand."

"Err, okay." Carl did as Sahir requested.

Sahir withdrew a dime, placed it in the palm of his hand, and showed it to Carl's friends. "Please don't take your eyes off the coin." Sahir moved his hand slowly, keeping it flat so that the coin was visible right up until the moment he embraced Carl's hand. He asked Carl, "Can you feel the dime?"

Carl nodded. "Yeah, of course."

"Excellent. I'd like us to shake hands and then, after the count of three, quickly turn our hands flat so that your friends can see our palms."

It happened exactly as Sahir had requested, and Carl's friends gasped when they saw the coin had vanished.

Carl rubbed his head, dumbfounded. "Well, I'll be damned. That's some trick."

Sahir bowed and said, "My sincere gratitude." He walked to the homeless man, who was forty yards away and out of sight of Carl and his friends, and dropped Carl's Rolex watch and wallet in the man's lap.

Sixty minutes later, he entered a tiny rental apartment in D.C.'s Upper Northwest. The place was clean and pleasant, but also cheap, nondescript, and one of many in the block. Unlike Sahir, who'd chosen the accommodation because it was discreet, occupants of the other apartments had a tight budget in common, but otherwise they were a diverse bunch of tourists, summer students, and employees on temporary assignment to the capital. Most of them took no notice of each other, and the only person

Sahir had spoken to was his neighbor—a young and pretty Argentinian woman called Isabella, whose parents had paid for her to come to the States to improve her perfectly adequate English, when in fact she seemed to spend most of the day in her apartment smoking weed. Isabella thought Sahir was a PhD student from the Bengal Engineering and Science University who was participating in a Georgetown University summer semester. She had no inkling that her neighbor might be a man capable of murder.

He entered the kitchen and opened a bag of masala peanuts while listening to Mr. Conrad and The Excellos sing "I'm Dissatisfied" on a CD he'd earlier purchased from the blues section of a record store because he wanted to understand how it was possible for American musicians to be unhappy in the land of hope and glory.

Six spiced peanuts, juggled high into the air before landing in quick succession in his mouth, abated all feelings of hunger, and he moved to the living room, opened a trunk containing chains, ropes, saws, shackles, and a razor wire whose sole purpose was to garrote a man, and withdrew a leather pouch containing sterilized needles of varying widths. He pulled out one that had been used by early-twentieth-century Quaker explorers to insert stitches into the paw of an injured tiger, and thrust the needle through the same palm that had earlier held the dime. Avoiding bones and veins was key, and as Sahir saw its tip emerge through the top of his hand, he imagined an audience who would be disgusted yet fascinated by what he'd done but wouldn't see the real reason behind the grotesque act, which was to increase his pulse rate to that of a frightened animal, sweat, and appear to everyone that he was a victim of his own machismo when in truth he was calculating facts about his emotionally vulnerable audience so that he could use their secrets against them.

Just like he'd done when he'd been a captive in the U.S. base in Afghanistan.

He closed the trunk and smoothed his hand over its surface. The sturdy piece had been handcrafted by him, and he was pleased with the result, because he was sure that there was no other trunk like it in the world. The box was large enough to contain a big man, and Sahir had designed it so that even he would be unable to escape the container if he was locked inside it.

Will Cochrane would slowly die in the coffin, chains wrapped around him, the garrote slicing his neck if he moved his head. It would be an agonizing death but one that was justified, because Cochrane had murdered his father.

Chapter 6

ON MY FIRST day of special forces airborne training in the Groupement des Commando Parachutistes, a jump instructor told me that my existing Foreign Legion qualification as a static line jumper meant shit compared to what he was going to teach me.

In his Gauloises-gravelly voice, he said, "Caporal Cochrane: The only way you can die during a static line jump is if you're shot while descending. Free-fall jumps are different because you have a one-in-thousand chance of your chutes not opening." He winked at me when he added, "I've got seven hundred and forty-one jumps under my belt, and so far my chutes have opened every time. But I'm getting closer to jump one thousand, and that means each free fall is taking me closer to death."

As I drove my newly acquired rental car west, away from D.C., I pondered the instructor's observation and decided that it had parallels to my existence, because statistically, one day I would fail. It had to happen—confronting a person who's smarter and more proficient than me, making a wrong decision, hitting a stroke of bad luck, or simply giving up the will to keep fighting. Of course, I'd no crystal ball or sixth sense to predict when that day would be. But I knew with certainty that I wouldn't die of old age, and that every day I went to work brought me closer to that one thousandth jump.

Maybe that day would be tomorrow, sometime after Trapper called me at 10:00 p.m. Or perhaps it would be today, because the man I was driving to see was a blood-thirsty lunatic who was a ten out of ten on my scale of nasty people I've had the displeasure to know. But I had to meet with him because he was a former Pakistani intelligence officer who had a brain the size of a small planet and the memory of an elephant, and knew pretty much all there was to know about terrorists in Afghanistan. And that meant he might know something that would help me nail the identity of Trapper.

Aside from his psychopathic tendencies, two things were against my winning over his cooperation: the first was that I'd outwitted him by setting him up to look like a CIA spy, forcing him to flee from Pakistan and its Inter-Services Intelligence agency for fear of being executed; the second, that shortly after his arrival in the States I'd had to plunge a knife into his arm to stop him from strangling me.

I hadn't seen him for five months and eighteen days, and I'd cherished our time apart. *But all good things come to an end,* I thought as I stopped my vehicle at a remote farm in Jefferson National Forest. This was his home, chosen for him with care by the CIA because the Agency didn't want him to cohabit too close to other citizens and stupidly hoped the stunning location might placate his egregious desires. I knew it would have the opposite effects. Isolating him gave him space to breathe and kill—since he arrived here, West Virginia had suffered eleven unexplained murders—and seclusion would enhance his warped but clear thinking in the same way that humbler men gain greater understanding of the world by becoming monks and retreating to monasteries. But Langley thought it knew best, and I was ignored by the bureaucrats who made these decisions and had never been up close and personal to thoroughbred evil.

Part of me wanted to put the car in reverse and get the hell away from here, but there was no point. Our meeting was by prior arrangement, he knew I was here, and I would have been dead by now if he wanted me to be.

I got out of the car and walked over the yard toward a huge clapboard farmhouse that was encircled by outbuildings and dense woods. I wanted the man I was meeting not to be an operative who'd once stood in an interrogation cell in Islamabad, recited W. B. Yeats's "He Wishes His Beloved Were Dead," and slashed a naked Islamist terrorist's stomach. But he was that person, as well as a craftsman of beguiling wooden toys, a student who'd taught himself the Choctaw Native American language in four weeks, an academic who'd deciphered the book of Revelation, a proficient anesthetist, and a man who could easily bench-press a three-hundred-pound frozen human torso.

As I knocked on the door, I told myself that I was nothing like him, even though I suspected that we'd killed nearly the same number of people, had identical intellects and espionage talents, and were only differentiated by purpose and sanity.

He called out from somewhere in the house. "Come in, Mr. Cochrane. My door is always open to you."

Instinctively my hand moved to my concealed sidearm, just to check it was still where it should be and to give me slight reassurance that I might walk out of this place in one piece. As I moved through the property, I noticed the interior had changed since I was last here. Back then, the home had been undergoing reconstruction and decoration; now it looked like the interior of a sheik's palace.

I had no idea where he was, but I soon found out. As I entered a large living room, I saw him sitting in the center of an expensive Oriental couch that was big enough to seat eight adults. He was barefooted, his legs in the lotus position, and he was wearing black trousers and a collarless white shirt and was grinning with ivory-white teeth. I guessed most women would find him sexy in a back-in-the-day-Omar-Sharif kind of way.

"Mr. Cochrane," he said in an accent that suggested he might have served as an officer in Her Majesty's Colonial Service, "are you hungry?"

"What are you offering?"

"Something unique."

"Then I'll pass." I sat in a chair opposite him. We were divided by an ornate Omani coffee table, on which sat a rare 1972 edition of *Playboy* magazine, his best-selling book about perpetual motion, a stuffed mongoose, and a dagger that I knew had once belonged to a disreputable Venetian prince. "Are you well?"

"Physically?"

I shook my head. "Mentally."

"You're prone to posing rhetorical questions?"

"I'm just breaking the ice."

"By asking about my mental health? You should learn some manners." The man, whose name was Zakaria, giggled like a successful prankster. "Why are you afraid?"

"I'm not."

"You are, as evidenced by a fact. What is that fact?"

"I'm armed."

"Correct. You bring a gun to my home; that's further testament to your bad manners."

We sat in silence for a while. I hated the quiet. Zakaria didn't.

When I could no longer bear the feeling that Zakaria was mentally raping me, I said, "I need your help."

Zakaria smiled wider. "Of course you do. But what do I get in return?"

I smiled back. "You get to keep living . . . here."

Zakaria glanced at the dagger. "How long are you intending to stay in the United States?"

"Not long."

Zakaria kept his eyes on the knife. Then he placed his manicured fingers together, dropped the smile, and locked his gaze on me. "Do you still fantasize about the erroneous possibility that your father might be alive, incarcerated in Evin Prison, a broken old man whose long hair and beard make him unrecognizable but one who's not dead?"

I was motionless because I didn't want to give the bastard the satisfaction of knowing that his question unsettled me. "He's dead. An Iranian general killed him in his prison cell after he was captured and taken to Tehran."

"My question doesn't pertain to the issue of whether he's alive or dead, but rather the fantasy."

"I know, and I chose to ignore it."

"Why?"

"Because you're a parasite."

"Always trying to categorize me, Mr. Cochrane. That's a flaw in you."

"Actually, I do it for fun and to annoy you."

"Rather crude objectives, don't you think?"

I shrugged. "I don't care. Keeps me happy." This was true. Baiting Zakaria was the only good thing about being in his presence. I repeated, "I need your help."

"And if I don't acquiesce, you'll kill me?"

"Maybe, or perhaps I'll tell the feds that the CIA is illegally harboring a very dangerous criminal." I swept my arm across the room. "Let them take you away from all this luxury, and watch them put you in solitary confinement. For life."

Zakaria laughed. "That would mean you'd have to step out of the shadows in order to testify against me. I can't see you liking that one bit."

I nodded. "Well, I guess that just leaves the option of killing you."

The glisten in Zakaria's eyes vanished, replaced by a darkness that made me wonder if I'd gone too far. To my relief he asked, "What help do you need?"

I leaned forward so that I was closer to the dagger if Zakaria attempted to grab it. "A young Indian man who calls himself Trapper wants me dead." I gave him what little data I had. "I'm wondering if you might know him, or know of him?"

"I wish him good luck." He tossed his head back and stared at the ceiling. "Appearance?"

"Slight, but wiry and strong."

"What is your colleagues' assessment of his intellect?"

"They thought he was clever."

"Demeanor?"

"Brave."

"And what is your assessment of your colleagues?"

"I think they're dumb and cowardly."

Zakaria drummed his fingers on his thigh. "Of course they are. And that means they're not credible assessors of a man's character. That said, perhaps by chance, or more likely because their stupid brains realized they'd been outmaneuvered, on this occasion they're right."

"I agree."

"I'm glad you do." Zakaria's smile had returned. "Trapper's an educated man, privileged, yet courageous and an independent thinker. What does that tell you?"

"He comes from a wealthy family, but I suspect he's been alone for some time; had to make decisions on his own."

"And therefore . . ."

"He no longer has a family."

Zakaria bared his teeth. "Heartbreaking, isn't it?"

"Not to you."

"But it is to you, for obvious reasons."

"Shut up and keep thinking and talking."

"Tut tut, Mr. Cochrane. Do you always feel the need to expedite our conversations?"

"Yes. You're mad, so I need to keep your mind on track."

"Your track, not mine." Zakaria lowered his head and looked at me. "Trapper is an unusual nom de plume, don't you think?"

I agreed.

"What image does it conjure in your head?" Zakaria was looking at me with his professor look.

I indulged him by pretending to be his student. "Many. Mark Twain. Old America. Frontier land. Guys in bearskins trying to survive alongside meandering rivers. Nothing remotely South Asian."

"And what can you extrapolate from that?"

"The code name's been chosen with care. It's specific to geographical location and me."

"Indeed, it is." Zakaria flicked a finger against the fangs of the dead mongoose. "I don't know who he is."

I made no effort to hide my disappointment.

Zakaria placed an electronic cigarette in his mouth. I was surprised, because he'd always been a devout smoker of Balkan tobacco. "You know what that means?" he said.

"It means he's not who he says he is."

"Probably, though new terrorists appear all the

time. Even I can't be expected to keep up with all their identities."

"But you believe Trapper has the wrong profile to be a terrorist?"

"I wouldn't be so bold as to make such an assumption. But I do think there's more to this than meets the eye. *Your* eye."

"And your eye?"

I knew Zakaria wasn't going to answer me.

Instead, he checked his watch and said, "I've told you the truth that I don't know who Trapper is. Do you feel that I've in any way been uncooperative on that point to the extent that I need to be incarcerated or murdered by the *great* Will Cochrane?"

"No. You've done what I've asked of you."

"Good." Zakaria stood. "I'm afraid our time's up, because in one hour I need to be fifty miles away from here to have a rather forthright chat with a man who owes me money."

I tried to object, but Zakaria raised his hand. "I hope I see you soon, perhaps under different circumstances. But for now, I'll leave you with one observation."

I was silent.

Zakaria's grin was back on his face. "The fact that Trapper wants you dead isn't your biggest problem. What should concern you the most is that he's told your colleagues and you that he wants that outcome."

Chapter 7

SAHIR WAS SITTING in his room, deep in thought. He needed to kill Will Cochrane. But he'd been told that it would be an exceptionally difficult task to capture him, let alone extinguish his life. And that meant he had to stack the odds in his favor by exploiting Cochrane's only vulnerability: his unwavering need to protect the weak and innocent.

Sahir's plan was simple and brutal, and—given the fact that Cochrane had murdered his father—it was apt that his father had inadvertently supplied him with the inspiration for the plan.

As a child, Sahir had sat on his father's knee and listened to his tales about their forefathers' exploits in India and elsewhere. He'd learned about a captain who'd served in the ranks of Queen Victoria's army and fought the Pashtun clans at the Khyber Pass, an architect who'd designed and built bridges over treacherous ravines in the mountainous north, a doctor who'd cycled the entire length of India to meet his future wife, and an owner of a tea plantation in Darjeeling who'd one day decided to diversify and cultivate opium.

The man who fascinated Sahir the most was his great-grandfather. Only one known photograph had ever been taken of him, and for the most part Sahir kept the photo on his person whenever he travelled. He pulled it out of his wallet and looked at the sepia image of a handsome yet roguish-looking man who was holding a rifle in one hand and a gin and tonic in the other, with a cigarette fixed in one corner of his smiling mouth and one foot planted on the head of a dead black leopard.

His name was Baber, but Sahir hadn't thought of him by that name ever since his father had talked about him. "He was a shikari! The last of his kind; the best shot in India. And when he died, no man had equaled his bag of tigers."

Shikari was another name for "hunter."

Sahir loved one story about Shikari his father had told him. He could hear his father's voice and words now.

"After World War I ended, he returned to his family home in Rajasthan, took off his Indian Army uniform, and told his village that his experiences on the Somme were nothing like hunting; he declared that any fool with a gun could have killed the poor souls who were sent over the top of the trenches into no-man's-land.

"His wife, children, and the locals in his village were scared of Shikari because they thought they saw madness and vulnerability in his eyes. But they were also scared for another reason: a huge tiger had been spotted in the nearby outskirts of the jungle. Determined to allay their fears and to prove to them that he was the man they knew before the war, he put on some robust silks, fixed himself a flask of gin—for he was a prodigious drinker by then— paid a villager for her goat, and took the leashed animal to the jungle, where he tied the goat to a tree and clambered up its branches.

"He waited there for two days, his rifle in his hands, never moving from the branch. The tiger came on the third night, its nostrils flaring. Shikari had never seen one so big and knew it was powerful enough to leap up the tree and rip him apart. But it was fixated on the tethered goat, whose gullet had been slit so that the scent of blood would make the tiger insane with hunger.

"The tiger moved closer, ready to kill the goat.

"Shikari glanced at the stars, aimed his rifle, pulled back the trigger, and shot the beast in its paw."

The child Sahir had interjected, "He missed?"

His father had shaken his head. "No. Just before the shot, Shikari had an epiphany that broke his heart. He realized the tiger was in no-man's-land and that he was no better than one of the enemy German machine gunners at the Somme, waiting for him and his Indian and British comrades to draw closer so that they could be mowed down.

"After the tiger limped away and collapsed, Shikari returned to the village with tears in his eyes and alcohol coursing through his body.

"His family and the villagers kept their distance

from him as he carried on drinking through the night. But his youngest son, your grandfather, was brave enough to knock on his door the next morning and tell him that a group of Quaker explorers were taking refreshments in the village and had heard he'd injured a tiger. They wanted to help the animal. The boy had expected Shikari to hurl drunken abuse at him, but instead he staggered to his feet and guided the Quakers to the spot where he'd last seen the injured animal. The tiger was still there, lying on its side, breathing fast. Using poles with nooses, they pinned the animal down, removed the bullet, cleaned the wound, and used needles to stitch it up.

"Keeping their guns trained on the tiger, they backed away and watched it limp into the jungle, never to be seen again. After the men returned to the village, the Quakers gave Shikari the leather pouch containing the needles they'd used to heal the tiger, and told him that they were to be his reminder that there was peace in the world.

"But Shikari knew he could never be at peace, because his life of hunting now seemed wholly wrong. So he gave the needles to his youngest son and went to bed, no longer a shikari, instead a confused and anguished shadow of his former self. That night, he died with the sound of German artillery fire raging in his ears."

Sahir placed the photo back in his wallet and imagined the tethered goat. That's what fascinated him the most about the story, because it seemed such an effective method to lure an alpha predator to its death.

And though Cochrane would want to rescue the tethered bait rather than kill it, the principle was the same. But he'd need something far better than a goat to distract Cochrane long enough to be able to creep up on him.

Chapter 8

WASHINGTON, D.C.'S ILLUMINATED night sky was sodden as I drove across a bridge that was taking me closer to the center of American politics and the city where Trapper believed I was hiding.

I was tired, and a large part of me felt that my trip to see Zakaria had been a wasted one because he couldn't identify the man who wanted to kill me. But I was also puzzled by his last observation and kept trying to understand what it could mean. Zakaria never said anything for the sake of it; he'd seen something that I hadn't, and that in equal measure annoyed and frustrated me as much as my car's faulty seat-belt warning device, which had been pinging every second throughout my return journey.

I toyed with the idea of arriving unannounced at the safe house to tell Chrissie that my being away was fruit-less and in any case I'd like to invite her out for a nightcap. But in doing that, I'd be telling her that I'd failed and had come back to her with my tail between my legs. I couldn't bring myself to do that because I could imagine Chrissie smiling and saying something like, "So you're like all the other Agency guys who talk a good game, trying to get me into bed, but can't deliver the goods when it counts?"

Actually, I couldn't imagine Chrissie saying anything like that, but I could imagine her thinking something similar, so I decided that tonight I wasn't going to give her cause to believe I'm like some of the CIA guys she has to put up with. I wondered if Chrissie could be the one for me. She certainly made me feel good when I was in her presence. I momentarily fantasized about the two of us going on vacation together.

But I quickly put that fantasy and all other thoughts about Chrissie out of my head. Capturing or killing Trapper was all that mattered right now.

I drove through the city, windshield wipers on full, scrolling through radio stations until I settled on one playing modern jazz, but I quickly turned it off because the music sounded discordant and illogical alongside the infuriating and robotic *ping ping* of my seat-belt warning system. Plus, I had to stay focused on road signs, because I didn't know my surroundings. Despite being a joint MI6-CIA officer for years, this U.S. trip was only the second time I'd been to D.C. Whenever I meet Patrick and his peers in Langley, they quickly put me on a plane to London because they think that if I stay in the States too long, I'll cause them trouble. Given my current circumstances, it seems they are right.

I'd no particular destination in mind, though I had a

loose idea to traverse the city until I found its northern outskirts and, hopefully, a motel where I could pay cash for a room, charge my cell phone, strip down and clean my handgun, and sleep. For now, I was an alien, drifting with buildings' lights flickering over my face, free-falling with no idea where I'd land, a lonely predator searching for a secure place to rest. Solitary spies often feel this way. The more seasoned of us might have visited most of the world's capital cities, but that doesn't mean we are knowledgeable tourists; instead, more usually we are furtive travelers who migrate at night from one country's Ritz Carlton to another's Hilton and have no connection to our surroundings beyond the fact that they hold a man or woman with the potential to betray their country.

I felt that way in D.C.

It was just another dark city.

It was close to 11:00 p.m. when I found a motel with neon signs advertising its forty-dollar rooms and inability to accommodate teenagers or truckers. As I hauled my luggage out of the trunk, I thought that there must surely be less desirable people that the establishment would wish to deter. For example, fugitives, murderers, and me.

I looked around, rain dripping off my face, and wondered if this was the last place I would ever sleep.

Chapter 9

AT NOON THE following day, Sahir slung a black canvas bag over his shoulder and stepped out of his apartment.

There were three other apartments that could only be accessed from the narrow corridor outside Sahir's apartment. As well as getting to know his immediate neighbor Isabella, Sahir had made it his business to ascertain the identities of his other neighbors. One of them was a construction worker who pulled twelve-hour day shifts and only came home to eat and sleep; the other was a sightseeing guide who spent every daylight hour walking tourists around D.C.

Sahir knew Isabella was in her apartment, because he could hear her singing along to pop music. As he knocked on her door, he wondered if she was stoned; he hoped so, because he wanted her to feel relaxed in his company. Not that he had any concerns about that, because Isabella struck him as the carefree, trusting type who saw the good in people rather than their flaws. Sahir liked that about her, and he was glad she was his closest neighbor.

"Who is it?" she called, probably panicking that the person at the door could be the landlord or a cop.

Sahir smiled. "It's your neighbor. I'm bored and wondered if you could make me a cup of tea. I've run out of anything to drink."

Isabella opened the door, a grin on her face, her eyes a bit bloodshot. "You're bored?"

"Yeah. Bored." Sahir made an effort to keep his attention fixed on her beautiful face and long hair, because he didn't want to appear rude as he was checking out her slender but curvaceous body, clad in hot pants and a tight T-shirt. "But if now's not a good time . . . ?"

Isabella frowned. "What's in the bag?"

"Nothing. I'm going to collect my laundry later." Sahir shrugged. "I'm trying to do anything to stop the boredom."

Isabella laughed. "I haven't got any tea."

"Ah, okay." Sahir half turned.

"But I've got Pepsi, milk, and wine."

Sahir's smile broadened. "A glass of milk would be good."

He followed her into her apartment. It was identical to his, though hers had cannabis smoke hanging midair in the living room and a coffee table with long cigarette papers, loose tobacco, cannabis resin, a bottle of red wine, and a half-empty glass.

Isabella gestured to the couch and turned the music down. "I'd have cleaned up if I knew you were coming over."

Sahir shrugged and lied, "Doesn't bother me. I used to be a big pothead. Only reason I'm not anymore is because I once got busted at my university and they threatened to kick me out."

"They're not here now. I won't tell if you want to share."

"Tempting, but I've got to finish an essay. I need a clear head."

"I don't." She sat opposite him and picked up a cigarette paper. "Do you mind?"

"Not at all. Actually, I enjoy being around smokers."

Isabella sprinkled tobacco in the paper, unsealed the resin, lit a match, and held its flame against the cannabis. Then she rubbed her thumb and forefinger against the singed area, turning it into crumbs, which she peppered over the tobacco. She placed a rolled-up piece of cardboard at one end, ran her tongue along the paper's adhesive edge, and sealed the joint. Putting it down, she went to the adjacent kitchenette, poured a glass of milk, came back, and handed it to him. After lighting the cigarette and inhaling deeply on the drug, she sat back down and asked, "You sure you're here just for a drink? You seem like a nice guy, but I don't want you to be disappointed, because I'm not the kind of girl who . . ."

Sahir raised his hand. "And nor am I that kind of man. Really, I'm just glad of some company. This essay's driving me nuts."

This reassured Isabella. "I hope this doesn't sound wrong, but I'd never met an Indian guy before you moved in here."

"And I'd never met a lady from Argentina before." Sahir winked at her. "We have crossed borders, have we not? And there can be nothing wrong with that."

"I agree." Isabella screwed her eyes up as she took another drag. "So, when you finish your PhD . . ."

"*If* I finish it."

"*When* you complete it, are you hoping to be an engineer or something like that?"

Sahir took a sip of his milk; it tasted off, but he gave no indication that it was bad. "I don't know. My parents want me to build things, though I'm not so sure. It's not my passion."

Isabella nodded. "Parents can be asses like that. Mine want me to be a teacher. I can't think of anything worse." She leaned forward. "What is your passion?"

Sahir placed his milk on the coffee table, adjacent to Isabell's drug stash, and let his hands drop to a position that looked natural but also kept them just out of sight. "Magic."

"Magic? That doesn't exist."

"Are you sure?"

Isabella shrugged. "I think so. Yeah, I'm sure."

"What do you think magic is?"

Isabella shrugged. "Stuff like creating fairies who live in the bottom of a garden. Or men claiming they can disappear in a puff of smoke."

"They can, and that's my point." Sahir moved his fingers quickly yet accurately as he kept his eyes on Isabella. "Fairies aren't real, but in 1917 two young English girls took photographs to show that fairies lived in their garden. People believed them. Magic became true." He nodded toward Isabella's latest waft of cannabis. "And smoke can hide a multitude of sins."

"They're just tricks."

"I prefer to think of it as misdirection. The girls took fake images of the fairies via a medium that, at the time, was deemed incorruptible—namely, photography. And the man who vanishes behind smoke is leading his audience to believe that the smoke is like his soul and can take vacuous form, when in truth it's a shield from which he can quickly retreat and hide before it clears."

"They're still just parlor tricks as far as I'm concerned."

"You have a point." Sahir placed a hand on the coffee table. "Real magic is amazing science in the hand of a person who knows what he's doing."

Isabella laughed, then coughed, while looking at her joint. "That's the kind of thing I might say when I've had too many of these. It's all a bit . . . ethereal."

Sahir swallowed the rest of his rancid milk. "Magic must be tangible for it to be recognized as such. Otherwise it's just unexplained phenomena."

Isabella topped off her glass with red wine. "Amen to that, and I've seen no evidence of the tangible."

"Yes, you have."

"Where, when?"

"Here, and now."

"What do you mean?" Isabella was staring at him, her eyes now lucid and inquiring.

"The cigarette you're holding. It tastes like marijuana, doesn't it?"

"Of course. It's a joint."

"And yet it has no marijuana or indeed anything else narcotic in it apart from nicotine."

"What . . . ?"

"Stub it out and see for yourself."

Isabella did what she was told; she ripped open the joint, held its remaining contents to her nose, and exclaimed, "That can't be possible!"

"I know. But here's the cigarette you rolled." Sahir moved both hands onto the coffee table, holding the joint.

She grabbed it and tore it open. "This isn't the joint I rolled. It's only got tobacco in it."

Sahir smiled. "Perhaps one of the two cigarettes on the bookshelf behind you is the joint you prepared."

Isabell stood and turned. "These weren't here before!" She tore them apart. "Tobacco, tobacco. No resin." She grinned as she pointed at him. "I've no idea how you put these here. Very clever, but still a trick. Not the joint I rolled. All you've shown me is tricks, not magic."

"Of course." Sahir placed the tips of his fingers together. "Would you like to know the true magic?"

Isabella nodded eagerly.

Sahir placed a digit on the rim of the ashtray. "Can you tell the difference between cigarette ash and ash from tobacco that's been combined with cannabis resin?"

Isabella was impatient. "Yes."

"Pinch the ash you see and smell it; taste it as well if you like."

Isabella did so and shook her head in astonishment. "That can't be possible."

"What isn't possible?"

"I smoked a joint that I rolled with cannabis resin inside. It turned out not to have resin in it, yet it produced ash that did." She was flummoxed. "How is that possible?"

"It's not. It's magic." Sahir tapped his empty glass. "Could I trouble you for another milk?"

Isabella burst out laughing. "Of course, sweetie. You know, you're great company. Stay as long as you like." She moved to the kitchen, holding Sahir's glass.

"I can't stay too long." Sahir followed her into the kitchen, yanked back her head, held her tight, and plunged a tranquilizer dart into her neck. "Not long now," he whispered. He dragged her backwards as she lost consciousness, then he forced her limp body into the black canvas bag.

Chapter 10

IT'S AN ODD tradition to give a condemned man a hearty last meal before a rope is put around his neck or he stands in front of a firing squad. I'd have thought his nerves would benefit far more from a packet of cigarettes and a bottle of Scotch. It's not as if he would need food to fuel his body, and I can't imagine a man would be hungry before death.

I wasn't hungry right now as I stared at my meal of steak, fries, and salad. No doubt the food in the diner was good. It *looked* good. But I just couldn't eat any of it. Instead, I sipped my black coffee while trying to come up with an excuse for the rather scary-looking waitress as to why I'd not touched anything on my plate. I toyed with the idea of telling her that I was unwell, or alternatively telling her the truth—that my name was Will Cochrane and tomorrow she would hear about my death.

I decided to take the cowardly route; I waited for her

to turn her back on me, left cash on the table, and walked fast out of the diner. I told myself I'd done this because I needed to retain every ounce of courage I had in case I needed to fight to save my life later on. It was horseshit. The truth was that nothing terrifies me more than scary women. That had been ingrained in me by, among others, a child-hating female instructor who'd taught me to swim by pushing my face in the water and pulling me out by my hair, Mrs. Eat Less, and an Irish woman from Killarney who'd loved making homemade bread and bombs.

It was raining hard and I was glad, because I didn't want sunshine right now. Good weather makes people happy, and I didn't like the notion that D.C. residents could be walking around with smiles on their faces on the day that I might die.

I got in my car, turned on the ignition, put my seat belt on, and muttered, "Fuck off" as the belt's warning system started doing its thing.

It was nearly 9:00 p.m.

Trapper was due to call me in one hour.

I drove into downtown D.C., left my car in a parking lot, pulled my jacket hood over my head, and got on foot for no reason other than the fact that I needed some air and time to think. I walked along a broad avenue and passed a block-long neoclassical government building with an endless row of columns illuminated for dramatic effect. But the beauty around me didn't register.

I wondered whether going after Trapper alone was the right thing to do when I could have easily availed myself of support from CIA paramilitary officers. But I was no different from most spies; we had to do things alone because it's how we'd been trained. You put a bunch of guys together, and you inevitably have a weak link. You let loose a spy, and he or she achieves tremendous success or dies. There's no in between, no weak link, nothing but uncompromising absolutes. And if you agree to accept a challenge and go out alone, there's no turning back; you have to keep going to survive. You march or die, as my seasoned Legionnaires would yell at me every day during the brutality of my basic training. March or die; spy or die. I'd traded one for the other and in doing so had jettisoned camaraderie in favor of solitude. I'd sought this, and I was seeking it right now, because I felt very angry and needed to get up close to Trapper, with no witnesses, in order to kill him.

I'D JUST RETURNED to my car when my phone rang.

"Mr. Cochrane?"

"Yes."

"You recall we had an appointment to speak now?"

I placed my hand over my handgun. "I do."

"Good." As ever, Trapper's English was well spoken, no hint of an Indian accent. Zakaria was right: Trapper came from a privileged background and had no doubt received his education at a school that believed that good intellect was impotent if combined with anything other than pitch-perfect diction. "Are you alone?"

"Always."

"Always? Oh, dear." Trapper sounded earnest when he said, "I know how that feels."

I wanted Trapper to get back to taunting me, rather than finding mutual ground about our sad backgrounds. "I'm glad you do. Why do you want to kill me?"

"Because you killed a senior Taliban leader who . . ."

"Bullshit. You're not Taliban or affiliated to them. This is cock and bull."

"Cock . . . ?"

"And fucking bull."

"My goodness, Mr. Cochrane, your language . . . Are you alone?"

"I'm alone."

"I do hope so, because if you're lying to me, things will go bad for you."

"I'm alone!"

"You're in D.C.?"

"You know I am."

"You have a vehicle?"

"I'm in one right now."

"A road atlas or GPS?"

"I've got both."

"Excellent. I want you to drive northwest, away from the city, and into the state of Maryland. Go to Germantown. Depending on your exact location in D.C., the journey should be no longer than one to two hours. When you reach Germantown, I want you to drive for another five or ten miles—I don't care about the exact distance, just so long as you find somewhere deserted and then stop and wait for me to call you with further instructions."

He hung up.

I drove out of the diner parking lot and headed out of the city on Route 270, while hoping I wasn't making an awful mistake.

SEVENTY-TWO MINUTES LATER, I reached Germantown and drove for another six minutes before stopping on the side of a deserted highway, amid featureless open countryside and farmland. Rain continued to pound my vehicle. All I could see was the few yards of road ahead, illuminated by my headlights. Everything else was pitch black.

I knew this wasn't the place where I'd die. Trapper had not been too specific about my route through Maryland and where I should stop. And I was certain I hadn't been followed here. No—this wasn't a kill zone; that place was somewhere else in Maryland. Soon I'd find out where it was.

I felt different from when I'd pursued Abram through the sewers. Then, I'd been totally unprepared for the possibility he wanted to kill me. But this was a premeditated moment. And though Trapper had the upper hand, we were both prepared for the probability that soon one of us would die. I'd been in situations like this before, and each time I had felt physically numb, mentally focused, and dislocated from everything that wasn't going to help me survive. Tonight was no different.

I waited, my engine idling, my seat-belt warning system pinging.

Nearly one hour later, Trapper called. "Are you where you're supposed to be?"

"Yes."

He gave me precise details for my next stop. "I will meet you there."

AFTER COVERING AN additional forty-two miles, I drove off the highway onto a rutted dirt track. More flat, open fields were on either side of me. There were no signs of any buildings, though it was so dark that it was impossible to know what lay ahead.

I passed a For Sale sign, and another one that told me I was on land belonging to Macquarie Farm. I drove for another hundred yards and stopped when the female voice belonging to my GPS announced that I'd arrived at my destination.

I thought, *No, I haven't; I'm in the middle of nowhere.*

But Trapper had given me an eight-digit grid reference to find him, meaning either my GPS was faulty, or I was exactly where I should be.

I was about to reenter the grid reference to see if it prompted the navigation system to guide me to another place, when my phone rang.

"I can see you, Mr. Cochrane. Don't worry: you're exactly where I want you."

I gripped my handgun. "Where am I?"

"I don't blame you for asking. Visibility here is poor to nonexistent at night. You're on a farm that for the last one hundred and seven years has been worked by three generations of the Macquarie family. For the majority of that time, the farm has produced very sizeable yields of corn. But the last owners were childless, and they recently died of old age. It's been empty and for sale for the last three years."

I got out of the car, my gun in one hand, the other holding my cell against my ear.

"Did I tell you to get out of the car?"

"No." I looked around, desperately trying to get my eyes to adjust to the dark. It was nearly a full moon, so I was confident I would be able to discern some features within minutes. Providing I wasn't shot before that happened. I spotted what looked like a pinhead of light in the distance.

"Have you seen it yet?"

I didn't respond.

"If you have," Trapper laughed, "then you've seen the light." His tone turned cold as he said, "Walk toward it, but stop when I tell you to."

I jammed my cell between ear and shoulder, and held my gun in two hands as I moved slowly ahead. I was in a field, one that previously would have produced hundreds of bales of corn per season. But now it seemed barren. I moved my eyes in a figure eight around the pinhead of light, trying to get night vision. If Trapper had me in the crosshairs of a sniper rifle, I'd be dead by now. Either he didn't have such a gun and needed me to get within range of whatever weapon he was carrying, or he wanted me to get closer so that he could attack me with something that would ensure my death would be slow and painful. I kept walking.

After approximately two hundred yards, the circle of light was a fraction bigger. As my eyes adjusted, I could see there was something in the distance beyond the light. It was on the horizon; maybe it was a solitary tree, or a building—I couldn't tell.

"Keep walking."

I did as I was told. The rain had abated, to be replaced by a fine drizzle; the air smelled of rotting grass. I asked Trapper again, "Why do you want me dead?"

Trapper hesitated before saying, "I suppose you deserve to know the truth. You killed my father."

"Your father? He was a Taliban leader?"

"No, he wasn't! He was an Indian man of impeccable standing in a community of fellow Muslims, but also Hindus and Christians. They loved him because he was a businessman who created jobs, a philanthropist, and a kind soul. You shot him in the head."

"I . . ."

"Shut up and keep moving."

Trapper's slow breathing was audible as I walked for another five minutes.

"Stop."

I did, and realized that my vision had fully adjusted to the night. Ahead of me, about fifty yards away, an oil lamp sat in the center of the field. Next to it was a trunk the size of a coffin. At the far end of the field was an old cylindrical wooden water tower, on top of a single thick stilt that was given further support by two diagonal ladders. A fenced walkway ran around the entire perimeter of the base of the tank. It was approximately three hundred yards beyond the lamp and trunk, and was an excellent place for Trapper to hide in while watching me through high-powered binoculars or something far worse.

The oil lamp was casting a golden glow over part of the trunk.

Trapper asked, "What do you think is inside the box?"

I pointed my gun at the tower. "Maybe nothing."

"Nothing?"

"Yes. Perhaps you want to put me in there. Suffocate me."

"Clever, Mr. Cochrane. I know what it's like to suffocate. It's the worst death. You deserve that. But let's presuppose that there might be something else in the box that's relevant to our . . . *situation*. What could that be?"

The lack of light made it impossible for me to see anyone on the tower. "Explosives," a thought occurred to me, "or bait."

"Bait. Excellent. What kind?"

"The human kind."

"Well done, sir. A radio mic is attached to the bait; I have the receiver. If I hold my cell close to the receiver, we can all communicate with the bait. Would you like that?"

"You bastard!"

"Because of you, I'm parentless. But I'm not a bastard."

"You are a . . ."

"Shush, shush. No time for that. Let's get bait on the line. Hello, bait."

I could hear a woman whimpering.

Trapper said, "Tell him your name."

"Isa . . . Isabella."

Trapper muttered, "Izzy Bella. You must be scared."

Her voice sounded muffled when she responded, "Please . . . please, let . . ."

"You go?" Trapper laughed again. "Not likely under current conditions. Mr. Cochrane: if you drop your gun, she might live. If not, she'll die because of your cowardice."

The numbness I felt earlier was gone, and my heart was pounding. "Who is she?"

"A twenty-year-old Argentinian girl with ropes around her body." Trapper sounded matter-of-fact when he added, "I can't really think of anything more interesting to say about her."

I took a step forward, my gun still pointed at the water tower. "Her voice could be a prerecording." Just like the woman's voice in the GPS that had brought me to this kill zone.

"Ask her anything you like, something I couldn't predict and prerecord."

My cell felt clammy against my ear. "She's still listening?"

"Yes."

My mind raced as I tried to think of a question that might resonate with a person who wasn't my gender or nationality, and was fifteen years younger than me. I decided to ask her to do something that was out of Trapper's control. "Isabella. Listen to me carefully. I want you to repeat back to me what I'm about to say."

Her voice sounded strained as she replied, "Okay."

"The phrase is: Trapper is seriously fucked up. I repeat: Trapper is seriously fucked up."

"I beg you . . ."

I shouted, "Just say it. It's proof of life and may just save your neck."

Isabella responded in a near whisper. "Trapper is seriously fucked up."

"Good." I asked, "Are you hurt?"

"Enough!" Trapper was back on the line and sounded angry.

I smiled. "Bet you didn't like that."

"I might as well kill you now."

"With a gunshot?" I took five steps forward. "Then you'll have failed to put me in the box."

Trapper was silent for a moment before asking, "Would you like to meet Izzy Bella? The trunk can be opened from the outside."

I stood stock still.

"Go on. If you're brave enough."

I walked quickly toward the trunk, knowing that if I fired my handgun, I'd struggle at this distance to hit the tower, let alone a man on its walkway.

I reached the trunk and saw that it was secured by numerous steel bolts. I'd no idea what Trapper's game was, but I had to open the trunk and get Isabella out of there. Keeping my gun pointed toward the tower, I slid back each bolt and swung the lid open.

What? I thought.

Inside was a young Indian man. He was bound in chains. Around his throat was razor wire that had cut into his skin. Blood had drooled out of his mouth; more of it covered his naked upper torso, having oozed out of a bullet wound in his chest. I placed my fingers against his neck, then his wrist. No heartbeat. He was dead.

The man at the end of the line said, "His name was Sahir. I told him you murdered his father and I could help him get revenge."

I tried to make sense of it. "Who was his father?"

"The man I described to you. Don't worry—you didn't kill him. I did. And tonight I killed his son."

I gripped my gun harder. "What is this about?"

Calmly, the man replied, "It's about a young man deliberately getting himself arrested in Afghanistan so that he could convincingly tell the CIA that you're being targeted for assassination. It's about flushing you out and doing so in a way that gets you on your own. And ultimately, Mr. Cochrane, it's about punishing you."

"For what?"

"One day you'll find out. Today's not that day."

I glanced at Sahir. He looked so young. "Did he know I was going to be here tonight?"

"Yes. He brought me the lamp, box, and sweet Isabella. He thought he was going to kill you. He was wrong."

"What are you? A terrorist?"

"Oh dear, no. I'm much more *special* than that." When he spoke again, his voice was deeper, and he sounded older. "Sahir and I are very different people—different nationalities, ages, backgrounds, and aspirations. But I let Sahir use my code name when he was in captivity so that you knew who you were dealing with. And I pretended to be Sahir when I called you. Misdirection. That's one thing Sahir and I did have in common. He was good at it. But I was better. I killed him after his work for me was complete."

"Why haven't you killed me?"

"I could easily do so right now if I wanted to. Instead, I prefer to punish you. And I'll keep doing so until I decide that you've suffered enough and need to be killed. But for now, you don't need to fear me. You've been punished enough tonight."

"Who are you?"

"I'm the real Trapper." He sounded like he was running. "Good-bye, Mr. Cochrane. We'll meet again."

The line went dead.

I shoved my cell into my pocket and ran across the field to the water tower, clambered up one of the ladders, and raised my gun. Isabella was sitting on the walkway, her knees bunched under her chin, ropes lashed around her wrists and ankles. A sock had been thrust into her mouth. I walked around the base of the water tank, poised to pull the trigger if I found Trapper. But he wasn't here.

I released Isabella from the ropes and gag. "Are you okay?"

"No . . . no, I'm not okay." She started crying.

"Are you injured?"

She shook her head.

"Where is he?"

"Gone, gone . . ." She lowered her head and started shivering.

"I'm getting help." I called Patrick, told him what had

happened, and ignored his yelling that it was the middle of the night.

He told me that he'd send a team of paramedics to help Isabella, an FBI agent who could ensure matters were kept quiet, and CIA officers who'd sanitize the place. He added that he wished I'd never been born.

I pulled Isabella to her feet, helped her get off the tower, and walked her across the field toward Sahir's coffin. I had her sit down where she wasn't close enough to see what had been done to Sahir.

I looked at Sahir, feeling sorry for him. He'd been duped by someone even smarter than him. It had cost him his life. But Trapper would have known that killing him was in no way punishing me. I didn't know Sahir. Nor did I know Isabella, and in any case, she was alive and unharmed.

None of this made any sense.

Chapter 11

THE FOLLOWING MORNING I drove back to the safe house to collect the rest of my belongings. Patrick and his team had left the farm thirty minutes ago. His CIA specialists had spent hours sanitizing the field of all traces of what had happened there. Paramedics had removed Sahir's body for cremation. The FBI officer had taken Isabella to a hospital, where she would be treated and monitored before being made to sign nondisclosure documents and flown back home to Argentina.

The sun was out and I was glad, because it meant I didn't have to worry about being killed. Plus, tonight I was going to take Chrissie out for dinner. When I'd asked Patrick about her, he'd told me that she was still at the safe house, adding, "Why wouldn't she be? She can't cover your ass from any other place." As I'd been about to leave the farm, he'd shaken my hand, given me the very slightest of wry smiles, and said, "Tomorrow, I want you on a plane out of here."

I knew Patrick wouldn't discipline Chrissie for helping me. She was too valuable to the Agency, and in any case I suspected Patrick was glad that I'd confronted Trapper and established that I was no longer under immediate threat. Patrick and my MI6 controller had told me that a big operation was looming and they needed me for the job. They couldn't afford to keep me in hiding much longer.

I stopped my car outside the safe house. It was the time of day when the ordinarily quiet residential street should have been showing some signs of life—people going to work or doing school runs. But it was dead. I decided that the occupants of the street *must* all be retirees who did nothing more productive all day than watch TV. I wondered if that's what I'd be doing in thirty plus years' time. I doubted it.

I was delighted to see that Chrissie's car was outside. If she wasn't already awake, I'd start cooking some breakfast to entice her downstairs—play housewife, as she called it; prove to her that I was a modern man who's good around the house.

I unlocked the front door and entered the house. The kitchen radio was playing samba music, so Chrissie must be up, I thought. I imagined her shamelessly wiggling her hips in time to the beat and then stopping and feeling a bit embarrassed when I caught her. "Honey, I'm home," I called out.

She didn't answer. *Music's too loud*, I thought.

I removed my jacket and decided that I needed to take a long soak in the bath. I felt grimy and didn't want

Chrissie to have to hang around a man who'd spent the whole night in clothes sodden with rain and sweat.

She wasn't in the kitchen; she was probably taking a shower. Damn. Now I had a mental image of her naked.

I made myself a black coffee and tried not to burn my mouth as I drank it fast to get a much-needed hit of caffeine. I felt exhausted; no doubt I needed at least a couple of hours' sleep in the safe house before we went out tonight, or I stood no chance of being good company over dinner. And I'd need to be at my very best, because apparently tomorrow I was on a one-way ticket out of town.

My back was hurting; I walked toward the living room so I could finish the rest of my coffee resting on the sofa.

Then my world turned over. "No," I yelled.

My hand involuntarily released the coffee mug.

Wearing a bathrobe, Chrissie was sitting on the sofa. Dead.

I ran to her, threw myself onto my knees, grabbed her limp hands, and repeated, "No, no, no! Chrissie: no!"

There were two bullet holes in her forehead.

Tears were running down my face, though I was barely aware of them. I was giddy from shock and felt like I was going to vomit. I sat next to her, cradled her head, and rested it against me while rocking her. Between sobs, I asked, "Who did this to you? Who . . . who could do this to you, my Chrissie? My . . . Chrissie."

I was overcome with grief, and I just held her, not knowing what to do. I cursed myself for leaving her here alone, for thinking this house was safe, and now finding her . . . like this.

She was cold but not in full rigor mortis, meaning she'd been murdered sometime during the night.

Sometime while I'd been out looking for Trapper.

I had to force my grief to one side and get my mind to focus. I pulled out my handgun and searched the house. But no one was here. I sat back down next to Chrissie and recalled what Zakaria told me.

The fact that Trapper wants you dead isn't your biggest problem. What should concern you the most is that he's told your colleagues and you that he wants that outcome.

And I remembered what Trapper told me last night.

It's about flushing you out and doing so in a way that gets you on your own. And ultimately, Mr. Cochrane, it's about punishing you.

Punishment.

Zakaria had suspected I was being taunted by Trapper so that I'd go after him. But I now realized he also suspected that Trapper wanted me to go after him because in doing so I'd leave behind people I care about. One of those people was the real target. I went after Sahir. Trapper killed him to keep his mouth permanently shut about their collaboration. And then Trapper went after Chrissie.

To punish me.

I felt like a fool.

And I had no idea how Trapper had gotten my cell phone number and the location of the safe house, and established that Chrissie and I were getting close. Nor did I know who Trapper was and why he was doing this to me.

That had to change.

I had to make Trapper pay for what he'd done.

But for now, I could no longer ignore my grief. I kept hold of Chrissie's hand. She was dead because of me.

Dead.

I tried to clear my head, telling myself that I should call Patrick. But he'd come over here straightaway and sanitize the place. I knew it had to be done, but now I wanted a few moments with Chrissie before my life was completely erased from hers. I reached into my pocket, withdrew a tiny box, and flicked it open. I removed the pendant I'd bought for her yesterday, placed it in her hand, and brought her fingers over it.

I wanted her to hold on to it for as long as possible.

More tears ran down my face as I kissed her on the cheek and whispered, "Good-bye, my love."

Acknowledgments

WITH THANKS TO my wife for being such an enthusiastic proofreader of my book; to my two brilliant mentors, David Highfill and Luigi Bonomi, and their second-to-none teams at William Morrow/HarperCollins publishers and LBA literary agency respectively; and to the lovely estate in the Scottish Highlands for enabling me to have the solitude to complete this novella amid inspirational surroundings.

Keep reading for an excerpt from

Dark Spies

the next installment
in Matthew Dunn's
thrilling Spycatcher series
Coming in hardcover October 2014
From William Morrow

ONE

Prague, 2005

IT WAS NO easy task to identify a spy and make that person betray their country. But that was what the Russian man was here to do.

Wearing a black tuxedo, he entered the InterContinental hotel's Congress Hall and fixed a grin on his face so that he looked like every other insincere diplomat who was attending the American embassy's cocktail party. There were hundreds of them, men and women, beautiful, plain, and ugly, from at least forty different countries. The less experienced of them were huddled awkwardly in small protective groups, pouring champagne down their throats to ease the pain of being here.

The Russian wasn't interested in them.

Instead he was here because he wanted to watch the

people whom he termed "the predators": the seasoned, clever, heads-crammed-full-of- juicy-secrets diplomats who glided through events like these, moving from one person to another, offering brief, charming, inane comments, touching arms as if the act conveyed profound meaning, before floating effortlessly to the next person. Diplomats called it "working the room," but the Russian understood that wasn't what they were doing. They were controlling the room and everything within it, watching for a moment when they could snatch a vital piece of information from someone weaker than themselves, or choosing the right moment to speak a few carefully chosen words and manipulate vulnerable minds.

The Russian knew the predators, and some of them thought they knew him—Radimir Kirsanov, a forty-something, low-level diplomat who was on a short-term posting to the Russian embassy in the Czech Republic. The women in the room liked Radimir because he had cute dimples, sky-blue eyes, blond-and-silver hair that was styled in the cut of a 1960s movie star, and the physique of a tennis player—the kind of shape that was not particularly good or bad in the naked flesh, but that wore a suit with rapierlike panache. Plus, they thought his dim mind made their superior intellects shine. The men, on the other hand, briefly glanced at him with disdain, as if he were a brainless male model.

Radimir grabbed a glass of champagne from one of the dozens of black-and-white-uniformed waiters who were navigating their way across the vast room, dodging diplomats, and skirting around tables covered in immaculate starched white cloths kept firmly in place by heavy candelabra and artificial-flower arrangements. The Russian held the glass in front of his chest, with no intention of drinking from it, moved past a bored-looking string quartet, and walked into the party. All around him was the sound of laughter, manifold languages, and women brushing against men who were not their partners.

Radimir made sure he didn't glide with the confidence and precision of a predator. He wasn't supposed to have the skills to do that. Instead, he meandered his way across the room, smiling to show off his dimples. He stood in the corner, shifting his weight from one foot to the other, sometimes smoothing a hand against his suit, as if he were fidgeting because he was ill at ease and had sweaty palms.

For a while, people noticed him. Beautiful people get that kind of attention. But as with gorgeous art, there's a limited period of time one can stare at a good-looking person before it becomes boring. After thirty minutes, he was sure he was invisible.

He moved to another part of the room, not too far, just a few yards to the next table, where he could pick at some canapés and fiddle with part of the flower display. He kept his gaze low, as if to avoid the embarrassment of having to talk to someone cleverer than him. Thankfully, the demigods around him knew that Radimir was aware of his limitations, so they left him alone. It was the only good thing they did for him.

Holding his champagne glass with two hands so that he looked like an amateur at this type of event, he walked to another table, then another, then several more. Forty minutes later he returned to his starting point in the corner of the room. Poor Radimir, he imagined the pros would think if any of them had seen his awkward and pointless amble around the room, though he doubted any of them had noticed. The predators were moving up a gear, pouncing on late and desirable new arrivals, placing firm arms around them and guiding them to people they didn't know but just had to meet, cracking jokes, whispering in ears, kissing cheeks, flattering, nodding with sage expressions, and all the time acting to hide their agenda: pure lust for information.

The Russian placed his full glass on a table, leaned back against the wall, folded his arms, and smiled his very best pretty and dumb smile. He'd practiced the expression many times in front of mirrors and he was convinced he'd perfected the look. It was an expression that he hoped said, I'm resigned to the fact that my looks are all I have.

It kept people away. Even the ones who were as dim-witted as he was, because no one wants to stand next to a man who's as stupid as they are but four times more attractive.

Radimir momentarily closed his eyes.

When he opened them, he was the cleverest person in the room.

A man who was not called Radimir.

Instead, someone who was known to a limited number of people as Gregori Shonin, an SVR intelligence officer. And a predator with skills that were way beyond those of the other predators around him.

There was a third side to the Russian, one that did not carry the false names of Radimir or Gregori, one that was the truth, but right now that was buried so deep inside him that he gave it little thought. This evening, being Gregori undercover as Radimir was sufficient for what he hoped to achieve.

Gregori's huge intellect was processing a vast amount of data, all gleaned from his forty-minute walk through the room. Hundreds of voices and sentences, many of them in English, some in other languages he understood fluently, only a few in tongues he didn't understand or care about. He spent several minutes doing nothing more than deliberately forgetting most of what he'd heard. Ejecting the crap, was how he like to term the cognitive process. It was an arduous task, but necessary, because at the end of it he would picture himself standing in this huge room, not with hundreds of diplomats from all around the world, but instead with one or two officials who worked for countries he loathed and who'd said or done something interesting.

Something that suggested they had the potential to spy on his behalf.

He continued the process of ejecting. Introductions, pleasantries, small talk, lots of "How long have you been posted here?," several people lying about how beautiful the American hostess looked tonight, a few jaded comments about last week's G7 summit, bad humor, and a fairly amusing anecdote from an Italian diplomat about her experience at a Mongolian tribal feast. All crap.

Gregori stared ahead. The room was still buzzing at

full capacity, but in his mind he imagined that only one American couple was in the place. Both were predators. They were standing still, frozen in Gregori's radar as he walked around them, staring at their faces from different angles as he sought a glance into their eyes and their very souls.

The husband was an experienced CIA officer who'd previously been posted to the Agency's stations in London, Abu Dhabi, and Pretoria. He'd been in Prague for two and a half years and was due to return to Langley in six months. He was thirty-seven years old, no doubt smart and capable, and had met his wife while both were studying at Harvard. She too could have gone on to have an excellent job in government, though early on they had decided that the overseas life of an Agency spouse would preclude her having a career. So, she'd agreed to be the good wife, accompany him on his overseas postings, and support him in every way, and in return he could give her a couple of kids. But so far they'd been unsuccessful in having children.

Gregori was interested in them for two reasons. One was a hushed and angry comment made by the husband to his wife.

"Are you sure that's where you were this afternoon?"

The other reason was perfume.

The wife loved Dolce & Gabbana perfume, so much so that she would never step outside of her home without applying too much of it to her throat and wrists. At events like these, one didn't have to stand too close to her to smell the unmistakable rich scent on her skin. But tonight was different, because she wore no such scent. Where had she been this afternoon? Gregori thought through the possibilities. A place she'd gone to clutching the ball gown she'd collected from the dry cleaners. A venue where she could get dressed in comfort, fix her hair, and put on makeup that she'd brought along in her handbag. Some location that didn't allow her time to rush home before meeting her husband at the party. And she would have desperately wanted to go home when she realized she'd forgotten to pack her beloved perfume.

Where was that place? Like all top spies, Gregori used his instincts and imagination to fill in the gaps. Of course, that place was another man's home. The woman had been unfaithful to her husband. She'd dressed for the party after she'd made love.

Gregori smiled.

Her infidelity could give him leverage over her husband.

Perhaps it would make her husband betray the United States.

TWO

Norway, Present Day

WILL COCHRANE CROUCHED on the frozen ground, removed his gloves, and withdrew two metal tubes from his rucksack. Each tube was two and a half feet long, ten centimeters in diameter, and branded with the name of the fishing equipment manufacturer Orvis and a label denoting that one tube contained an eight-foot-four-inch mid-flex Helios 2 fly-fishing rod and the other contained a ten-foot tip-flex variant of the same precision distance-casting model. He laid the tubes side by side on the ground, pulled out binoculars from his jacket, and examined his surroundings.

The tall man was alone on a mountain escarpment along the stunningly beautiful northern coastline. Around him were large azure-blue fjords that cut through the snow-capped mountain range, low areas of barren land carved into numerous islands by thin stretches of seawater, patches of mist hanging motionless over sea and earth, and above him a windless clear sky that looked heavenly and yet was cold enough to kill an ill-equipped man in less than an hour. But there were no signs of life out here save for an occasional kittiwake bird gliding close to water.

Carefully, he moved his binoculars until he spotted an area of lowland through which a thin meandering mountain river led to the sea. It was an excellent place to cast a lure and tempt a salmon or sea trout. But it was approximately one thousand yards beneath him; one would need be dressed in appropriate clothing and be at the very peak of physical condition to reach the area and fish there at this time of year. Thankfully, Will was supremely fit and had come fully prepared to stay out all day in this remote place. He was wearing a white woolen hat that was pulled down tightly over his close-cropped dark hair, a jacket and fleece, thermal leggings and water-resistant pants, and hiking boots covered with rubber galoshes. In these parts, an angler needed to dress like someone who was hiking to the North Pole.

As he further examined the distant stretch of river, his vision locked on the only evidence that any person had been here before: three log cabins and a track leading away from them. He wondered if the owners of the buildings had long ago deserted this place, or whether the cabins were rented out to vacationers during the summer months. He imagined clambering down to the river, preparing one of his rods, and making a few casts before being confronted by an angry owner of the cabins who would be shouting at him to leave.

Still, it would be worth the risk to try to fish there, as it would be a once-in-a-lifetime experience.

But that experience would have to take place on another day.

Because the MI6 operative wasn't here to fish.

He unscrewed the caps on both tubes and withdrew pieces of metal equipment that had been designed and handcrafted by specialists in England before being couriered in a diplomatic bag to the British embassy in Oslo. Carefully, he slotted each piece together. One minute later, the sound-suppressed, high-velocity sniper rifle was fully assembled. After putting his gloves back on, he lay flat on the ground and stared at the buildings though the gun's powerful telescopic sight.

He spoke into his throat mic. "In position."

And immediately heard an American woman's voice in his earpiece. "Okay. We got you."

The woman was a CIA analyst, operating in the Agency's headquarters in Langley, and was temporarily seconded to the highly classified joint CIA-MI6 Task Force S, which Will worked for as its prime field operative. She wasn't very experienced, but didn't need to be, as today her job was simply to sit at her computer and make notes of what Will could see.

Getting on this assignment had infuriated Will because it had come on the back of his being told without explanation that he was to cease his hunt for Cobalt. He'd spent the last eleven months chasing the financier—a man without a name or identifiable nationality, but one of the most dangerous men on the planet due to his funding of terrorist activities across the globe. Cobalt was all the more dangerous because he had no causes beyond seeking profit; his support of terrorist cells bought him their allegiance and gave him access to opium and coca plantations under their control. He transformed the crops into salable drugs, used his extensive network to smuggle them out of the countries, made vast fortunes, and in return gave the terrorists a cut of the profits. It was a deal that suited him, and suited them. And it was one that ordinarily would require someone like Will Cochrane to put a bullet in Cobalt's brain. But the powers that be in Washington and London had decided that Cobalt needed to be left alone.

So here he was, on a routine job that should have been given to one of the Agency's many paramilitary Special Operations Group officers.

In the largest wooden building below was Ellie Hallowes, the CIA's best deep-cover officer. Will had never met her, but he knew she was thirty-five years old—the same age that he was now—and was an excellent and courageous operator whose job required her to live in near constant danger. Today, he was here to watch over her while she met a Russian intelligence officer who carried the CIA code name Herald. The Russian was her spy, and during the last two years they'd met many times without the need for protection. But this meeting was different. Two days earlier the CIA had received signals intelligence that suggested the Russian intelligence services had suspicions about their officer and the real reasons for his trips overseas. The Agency was worried that the meeting could be compromised and that Ellie could be attacked. If that happened, Will was under orders to do whatever was necessary to ensure Ellie escaped to safety.

It was a straightforward job for a man like Will.

As a younger man, he'd spent five brutal years in the French Foreign Legion, initially in its elite 2e Régiment Étranger de Parachutistes before being handpicked to serve in the 11e Brigade Parachutiste's Special Forces unit, the Groupement des Commandos Parachutistes. Upon completion of his military service, he'd returned to England and studied at Cambridge University. After being awarded a first-class degree, he'd briefly considered a career in academia, though others had different plans for him. MI6 tapped him on the shoulder and said it was very interested in someone with his skill set. He could have turned the intelligence agency down and hidden away from the world in an ivory tower, surrounded by books and with human contact limited to students and other lecturers and professors. But MI6 knew it was an impossible dream for someone like him: a man whose CIA father had been captured in Iran when Will was five years old and incarcerated in Tehran's Evin Prison for years before being butchered, who'd fled to the Legion aged seventeen after witnessing the brutal murder of his English mother, who'd killed her four assailants with a knife to protect his sister from a similar fate, who'd been deployed not only by the GCP behind enemy lines but was also used by France's DGSE as a deniable killer, a man who was not completely at peace with the world.

Within the first few weeks of training alongside other recruits, MI6 had singled him out as having attributes that were even greater than expected. He was removed from the course and put on the top-secret twelve-month Spartan Program. Only one person at a time was permitted to take the mentally and physically hellish selection and training course and, if successful, carry the code name Spartan. Despite the fact that all other applicants before him had either voluntarily withdrawn from the program, failed, received severe physical or mental injuries that prevented them from continuing, or died in selection and training, Will passed the program. He was awarded the distinction of carrying the code name, and the program was shut down and would remain closed all the time Will was operational and alive. He'd spent the subsequent eight years on near continuous deployment in hostile overseas missions, and was tasked on the West's most important operations. Throughout that time, very few people knew he was an MI6 officer, let alone the nature of his work and his achievements.

He sighed, concluding once again that today's baby-sitting job should have been given to someone else. After slotting a magazine containing twelve rounds into the rifle, he trained the weapon on the track leading to the cluster of buildings. That was the route Herald would take to drive to the meeting. He checked his watch. Ellie Hallowes was a stickler for exact timing, and she'd told the Russian that he was not to arrive a minute before or after the allotted time. The Russian wasn't due to arrive for another eight minutes.

Will relaxed and thought about other things. A year ago, he'd moved into a new home in West Square, in the Borough of Southwark, south London. It was a two-hundred-year-old house that had been converted into four apartments. For the first time in his adult life, it was a place where he felt he was putting down roots. A sudden panicked thought hit him. Had he paid the latest council tax bill? He thought he had, though—shit—he couldn't be sure. The local council was becoming a bastard with people who didn't pay up on time. Well, there was nothing he could do about it until he got home tomorrow. He thought about his three single neighbors who lived in the converted house: stubborn Dickie Mountjoy, a former major in the Coldstream Guards and now a retiree; Phoebe, a thirty-something art dealer and lover of champagne, high heels, and middleweight boxing matches; and David, a recently divorced, slightly flabby mortician. They believed Will was a life insurance salesman. That false cover seemed apt, because today he was here as insurance that Ellie lived.

He glanced at his watch again and put his eye back against the scope. A black sedan was driving along the coastal track, at exactly the right time, easily visible against the backdrop of the tranquil blue sea. Will moved his weapon millimeter by millimeter to keep the crosshairs of his sight in the center of the vehicle. It stopped, and a man got out and walked fast into the largest of the three buildings.

"Our man's arrived. He's in the building."

"You're sure it's him?"

"It's him."

He flexed his toes and his muscles. Not for the first time this week, he tried to decide if he could afford the nineteenth-century sheet music for Bach's Lute Suite No. 1 in E minor. It was for sale in a tiny basement store in London's Soho district. He'd paid the elderly proprietor of the store a £50 deposit to take the music temporarily off the market, with the promise that he'd settle up the balance of £750 after his next paycheck had come through. Still, as desperate as he was to place the sheets on a stand, pick up his German antique lute, and expertly play what was in front of him, he had to reconcile the high cost with the fact that he was a man who was on government salary, could obtain the same music for free at a library or off the Internet, and in any case knew every note of Suite No. 1 by heart. But the score had been produced and edited by Hans Dagobert Bruger, meaning the papers were a rare and beautiful thing. That was decided then; he'd eat beans on toast for a month to ensure he had enough cash to pay for the sheets. Will had made many similar decisions in the past. His new home was crammed with antiques and rare items he'd picked up during his travels, including a Louis XV lacquer and ormolu commode, Venetian *trespoli*, a pair of Guangzhou imperial dress swords, a German chinoiserie clock, an Edwardian mahogany three-piece suite and chaise longue, woven silk rugs from exotic markets, and vintage vinyl records of Andrés Segovia guitar recitals. He shouldn't have bought any of them, because every time he'd done so he'd nearly bankrupted himself, but he'd always done so because life was too short to ignore beauty in favor of financial well-being.

He tensed as he saw movement in the distance.

A man walking awkwardly over rough ground, using a walking stick as an aid.

Will trained the scope on him and watched him move toward the cabins, stop approximately two hundred yards away from them, and sit on a boulder on ground that overlooked the cluster of buildings and the sea beyond them. The man had his back to Will, so his face was not visible, though Will could see that he was wearing tweed and oilskin hiking gear. His walking stick also seemed to be from another age; it was nearly as long as the man and at its head was a curly ram's horn. Judging by the way he'd been walking, it was clear that the man needed the stick, meaning he was either old, weak, disabled, or all of those things. The man rested his stick beside him on the rock, withdrew a metal thermos flask, poured liquid into a cup, and drank.

Will relayed what he's seen to Langley.

"Suspicious?"

"Impossible to know." Will moved his face away from the scope. "I'm going to look at his face."

Carrying his rifle in one hand, Will ran while keeping his upper body low. Two minutes later, he threw himself onto the ground, then crawled until he reached the summit and could once again see the distant cabins in the valley. The man was still there, a tiny speck to the human eye. Will looked through the scope, moved the gun until he located the man, and saw that he was still sitting on the rock. From this angle, Will could easily see his face.

He studied it, felt shock, and muttered, "Hell, no!"

ANTAEUS DABBED A handkerchief against the corners of his mouth to absorb any traces of the coffee he'd now finished, rested his weaker leg over the stronger one, and rubbed the disfigured side of his face before realizing what he was doing and abruptly stopping. It was a habit he'd had for years and he was trying to break it, because no amount of massage would get the muscles on that side of his face to work properly. His carefully trimmed beard helped to hide the lower part of the disfigurement, and the thick rims of his glasses covered most of the area where his left eye drooped. From a distance, he looked normal. But up close there was no mistaking what he was: a man who was ugly on one side.

He'd long ago gotten used to it and no longer cared. All that mattered to him was his mind. It was perfect and beautiful.

He stared at the Norwegian log cabins and gripped his walking stick.

The performance was about to begin.

And he was going to be its conductor.

ELLIE HALLOWES DESPERATELY wanted to cut to the chase and find out whether Herald had any useful intelligence for her, but knew that her Russian spy would consider it rude of her to do so. He was a showman, one who took pleasure in feeding her an hour or so of small talk before getting down to business. She was his audience, and he liked to keep her waiting for the good stuff.

During the third meeting she'd had with him after the start of their case officer–asset relationship, she'd tried to circumvent the crap to get to business, but had received a sharp rebuke from the Russian together with threats that if she did this again he'd come to the subsequent five meetings with zero of interest and plenty of lessons about how to be civil and conduct meetings in a manner befitting their respective countries' officer classes.

As well as being a showman, Herald was a pompous ass.

He was already thirty minutes into the meeting, sitting cross-legged in a chair facing her, occasionally glancing at his manicured fingernails or checking that his bow tie was horizontal.

She moved to the sea-facing side of the cabin and gestured to a bench containing a half bottle of vodka and two tumblers, while trying not to yawn as Herald was telling her that he'd discovered a fine restaurant in Moscow where all the staff were only permitted to speak in French.

Something caught her eye as she casually looked out of the window while unscrewing the bottle.

Movement in the sea.

Men.

Seven of them expertly emerged from the sea in scuba gear, dumping some of their equipment on the thin beach, and moved silently on foot toward the log cabins while keeping their SIG Sauer handguns at eye level.

Spinning around, she barked, "Shut up! We're compromised!"

Herald's face went ashen. "What?"

"Compromised! We've got seconds!"

Herald jumped to his feet and looked around, confusion all over his face. He walked quickly to Ellie, glanced out the window, grabbed Ellie's arms, and spoke fast and loud. "Listen to me! Trust no one. There's a mole in the CIA. Works for the Russians. And he's sitting at the very top!"

WILL'S HEART AND brain were racing as he spoke into his throat mic. "I'm looking at a man who's supposed to be dead."

"Who is he?"

"High-ranking SVR officer. Code name Antaeus. I killed him three years ago."

"Means nothing to me."

Will kept the crosshairs of his scope on Antaeus's head, placed his finger on the trigger, and made ready to put a bullet into the brain of a man who'd consistently outwitted the West's attempts to counter his actions; a man Will had spent years hunting, an individual who'd thwarted every attempt to neutralize him, a brilliant spymaster who was one of the Russia's most influential and powerful men. Until Will had finally managed to track him down three years ago and detonated a bomb under the car that Antaeus was driving in a Moscow suburb.

Will pulled back on the trigger.

Then stopped as he heard the unmistakable sound of pistol fire near the log cabins.

ANTAEUS SMILED AS he watched his Russian team approach the log cabins. He removed a small rectangular box from his jacket and withdrew from it a cheroot cigar, which he lit with a gold Zippo lighter. The doctors had told him that he mustn't smoke anymore, and for the most part he followed their instructions. But there were moments when a smoke made complete sense. Doctors didn't understand that; spies did, and now was one such moment. He inhaled the rich tobacco and blew out a long stream of smoke, the volume of which was accentuated by the icy air. As he did so, four of his men kicked in the doors to the two smaller buildings and entered; the remaining three operatives forced entry into the larger cabin.

Then he heard two shots.

Though he'd permitted his men to shoot to wound their targets if necessary, the SVR spymaster wondered if the CIA officer had made the shots the moment she'd seen men burst into the cabin, or whether her Russian agent had done so. Still, if two of his men were now dead, it wouldn't change anything. His other men would easily overpower the American woman and her asset. They'd dispose of their colleagues' bodies in the sea, but even if they were later discovered, that wouldn't matter, as Antaeus had instructed his men to use CIA SOG equipment and carry documentation showing they were residents of Virginia.

He tapped ash from his cigar, raised an old telescope to his good eye, and waited.

WILL POINTED HIS sniper rifle at the cabins and the ground around them. Two shots had been fired, but there were no signs of any assailants. He knew there could be only one possible explanation: men had assaulted the cabins from the one blind spot he had—the sea. Had he been complacent? He had considered the possibility that an assault on the meeting could take place from the coast, though had decided that at this time of year it would be done so with boats that would be easily visible to him from his position on the mountainside. Plus, he thought that no one in their right mind would swim in the icy waters to the coastline where the cabins sat. And yet, he of all people knew that Special Forces could operate in Arctic waters all year round. Yes, he had been complacent.

As a result, he'd probably failed a routine assignment that he'd believed was beneath someone of his capabilities. "Shots have been fired. Don't know what's going on. But I'll make sure Antaeus and his men don't leave here."

"Negative." The analyst sounded unsettled.

"What?"

"Repeat, negative. You have no authority to proceed."

Will couldn't believe what he was hearing. "I can do what I like."

The analyst sounded on the verge of panic. "I've checked our system. Don't know what it means but the instructions are clear. It says, Antaeus must not be touched. Further inquiries require Project Ferryman clearance. My search on the system must have been flagged, because I just had a call from the duty officer asking me what's going on. I told him. He told me to pull the plug. You're under orders to withdraw."

"No way."

"Your orders are clear. Get out of there."

"No fucking way!"

"I . . . ." The analyst was breathing fast. "I . . . the DO told me it would be a breach of category one Agency protocols if you proceed. Please . . ."

Men emerged from the smaller cabins and a moment later the rest of them came out of the larger building. Two of them were dragging Herald, and it looked as though he'd been injured. The others were gripping Ellie's arms and walking her to a clearing in front of the cabins. They stopped. The Russian was forced onto his knees and winced in pain as one of the men yanked his hair back to lift his head. Ellie was pushed to the ground next to her asset, and a man placed a boot on her back to keep her still. The men looked toward the distance. Will urgently swung his rifle toward Antaeus's position. He was still there, calmly smoking his cigar.

What was happening?

Antaeus was motionless for a moment. Then he lifted his stick high in the air.

Of course.

Antaeus had told his men that the he needed to be sure the Russian was the man he was after.

If he was, he'd give them a signal to proceed.

By lifting his stick.

"It's an execution!" Will swung his weapon back at the man holding a pistol against the Russian. But he was too late. Two bullets were fired into the back of Herald's head. His killer released his grip on the dead spy and let him slump face first toward the ground.

"Our asset's dead." Will gripped his gun tightly as he saw the man who was pinning Ellie to the ground lean forward, yank up her head, and look in the direction of Antaeus.

Will darted a look at Antaeus.

The spymaster was raising his stick.

Will trained his gun back on the man who was now lifting his gun toward Ellie's head.

"You're under orders to withdraw. If you don't, you'll be—"

"Enough!" Will pulled his trigger, and his bullet sliced through the Russian operative's eye and exited through the back of his head.

The remaining six operatives immediately sprang into action, five of them dashing for cover while one of them coolly remained still and raised his gun to complete Antaeus's orders to kill the CIA woman. Will's chest shot made that man flip backward. When he was on the ground, a second round smashed through his skull.

Ellie was crawling forward, staying low to give Will sight of her captors. But she was still an easy target for them. Will got onto one knee, fired five rounds at the areas of cover the Russians were using to remain hidden from his sniper rifle, ran fifty yards farther along the mountainside, got onto his knee again, and looked through his scope. The different angle put three of the men in his sightline. He took a deep breath, half exhaled, held his breath, and fired three shots in three seconds. Each bullet hit its target; the three men were dead.

He ran again, desperately hoping that the remaining two operatives could no longer see Ellie, then stopped and examined the area around the cabins. It was no good. The men were staying out of sight, and Will knew why: they stood no chance while Will was out of the limited range of their handguns; their best hope lay in forcing him to come nearer to them, to a distance where close-quarter pistols would be far more effective than a rifle.

Ellie was still inching away from the clearing in front of the cabins. No doubt she was waiting for the moment one or both of the men broke cover and shot her in the back. Will had to get to her, and fast, but while the men were still hiding there was one thing he had to do first. Kill Antaeus.

He pointed his gun at the area where Antaeus had been sitting.

The spymaster was no longer there.

Will urgently scoured the distant mountainside for signs of the Russian.

Nothing.

He silently cursed.

After fixing a fresh magazine into his rifle, he ran down the escarpment toward the buildings, leaping over clumps of heath that were renowned for twisting or breaking hikers' ankles, hearing the gentle whoosh of the sea grow louder as it eased back and forth over the seaweed-strewn coastline's pebble-and-sand beach, the rich and salty air causing his nose to sting and his lungs to feel that they had acid inside them as he sucked in the brutal air to fuel his exertions.

The cabins were now five hundred yards away, still too distant for the men to pose any threat to him. He slowed down as the incline lessened and he was confronted by round white rocks as high as his waist, haphazardly scattered on the heath as if dropped there from the heavens by playful child gods. Moving at a walking pace between them, he removed the weapon's scope and raised his rifle to eye level, using the fore and rear sights to try to spot the men.

Nothing.

Then he sensed movement to his right, and he flinched, crouched, twisted, and readied his gun. But it was only a white-tailed eagle, launching itself off the ground with a small writhing rodent in its beak. As the bird rose higher, it was able to glide with only the occasional flap of its majestic wings. Will recalled watching a similar bird of prey circling high above him in a remote part of Russia, while he was putting a brave, dead colleague's entrails back into his body.

He wondered why that memory had come to him now, of all times.

Was he about to die?

Maybe. On this routine operation. One that he'd believed was beneath him. What an idiot he'd been.

The CIA analyst spoke again, something about him having to surrender to CIA custody because he'd disobeyed orders, but her words barely registered. He turned off his radio and moved beyond the boulders onto flatter land.

He felt each step was drawing him closer to death.

He could see Ellie clearly now with his naked eye. She'd stopped crawling and was staring at Will with a calm expression. Most people in a similar situation would have bolted from the scene in fear. And they'd have been killed in doing so. But Ellie was very different; she knew exactly what she was doing.

Remain motionless.

Put her faith in Will.

Only attempt to escape if Will failed.

Will was two hundred yards away from the cabins. Though it would take a very lucky shot to hit him at this distance, his breathing was fast, and his temples throbbed.

And as he moved farther forward, he kept asking himself, Are you sure you paid that council tax bill? Really sure? Because if you haven't, you'll be summoned to court and will be fined a hefty sum that will preclude you buying anything by Hans Dagobert Bruger. He didn't know why this thought was in his head, but did know that thinking about it was far preferable to thinking about getting to within range of two men who'd kill him without hesitation or remorse.

One hundred yards.

Kill range for an expert shot holding a handgun.

God, was he facing such men? He was. Antaeus only surrounded himself with excellence, so the two men before him were no doubt expert operatives.

He walked toward Ellie, his gun moving left and right to cover the two areas beyond her where he thought the operatives were hiding—small grass-covered mounds that were fifteen yards in front of the largest timber cabin, places where at any moment two men could break cover and put bullets in his heart and brain. He'd never thought he would die in a beautiful place. Instead, he'd always believed it would be in a dingy hotel room, a war zone, or a Third World gutter.

He made a decision. If he died here, his soul would stay nearby, drifting along the rugged coastline and fantasizing about casting a line into one of the rivers as the Atlantic salmon made their run. It was a lonely place, yet stunning. He would be at peace here.

When he reached Ellie, he crouched beside her while keeping his gun fixed on the mounds. Her drawn face was covered in grime, though her eyes were glistening and focused. He made ready to move on, but she grabbed his arm and yanked down on his jacket.

She whispered, "Got a spare handgun?"

Will shook his head.

To his surprise, Ellie smiled, winked, and said, "Then there's a lot resting on you being able to do your job." Her expression turned resolute. "Good luck."

Will moved toward the cabins.

THE RUSSIAN SVR operative glanced at his colleague twenty yards to his left and nodded to indicate that he was ready. He didn't need to make the gesture, as both men had served together in numerous Special Forces and intelligence combat situations to the extent that they could read each other's thoughts in situations like this. They could operate anywhere—land, sea, air, rural, urban—but excelled in the places that could break an otherwise tough man. Though rugged and cold, this place was a walk in the park compared to the weeks-long training exercises and operations they'd done in Siberia and the Arctic Circle.

And it would be a pleasure and a mere formality to deal with the man coming toward them. Though the Russian knew snipers could be useful, he felt nothing but contempt for them. Killing a man from a distance was an easy thing to do; it was not until you'd experienced putting your hands around a man's throat and watching his eyes nearly pop out, or wrenching a knife upward in his belly while smelling his breath as you held the back of his head close to yours, or seeing a flash of fear in his eyes as you walked quickly toward him and made two shots into his chest, that you really understood what it took to extinguish a human life. Snipers rarely got their hands dirty. They didn't understand close-quarter combat.

The Russian and his colleague did.

He heard footsteps.

Now the footsteps were faster, the noise of them growing louder.

The sniper was coming for them.

The Russian raised three fingers to his colleague, then two, then one.

They broke cover from behind the mounds, their pistols raised toward the encroaching sniper.

But he wasn't there.

The Russian stopped and held his handgun before him, twitching it left and right to search for the sniper. Where had he gone? Movement from near the cabins to his left. He changed stance, pointing his gun in that direction, and for half a second saw his colleague being dragged backward while still upright, his feet desperately trying to keep up with the rest of his body because a big hand was on his throat, and another had two fingers in his colleague's nostrils. The rest of the sniper was obscured. His colleague was being used as a shield. The Russian had no clear shot before they disappeared into the largest cabin.

That's where the sniper had run to, and where he'd emerged from to attack their flank when they broke cover.

The Russian operative dashed to the buildings, entered the cabin, and saw his colleague on the ground, his neck at an odd angle and clearly broken.

He felt an almighty punch to his chest.

Another punch struck him on the jaw.

A hand slapped him in the throat.

A knee smashed into his ribs. His hand was grabbed, twisted so that his arm muscles were in a lock and were weak, and he was forced to the floor and held there in a viselike grip. He knew what was coming next.

Will Cochrane's boot slammed with brutal force into his throat and held him there as his legs thrashed and his life was crushed out of his body.

Before he died, the Russian's last thought was that he'd totally underestimated his assailant.

THREE

STANDING IN THE same spot where Will Cochrane had momentarily crouched beside her, Ellie Hallowes watched the tall officer emerge from the cabin holding one of the Russians' pistols.

He stopped and stared at the five men who'd died outside of the buildings. Ellie thought he looked haunted by what he'd done. That surprised her, because she'd met enough paramilitary men to know that they were totally focused while doing a job and acted like overexcited kids when the job was done. This man was clearly different.

He tucked the pistol under his belt, knelt beside Herald, rummaged through the dead spy's pockets, and removed his wallet and ID documentation, which he secreted in his jacket. She frowned as she watched him take off her asset's overcoat. It was the same one that

Herald always wore when he met Ellie during the winter months—knee-length, expensive, Royal Navy blue, hand-tailored in Savile Row by an émigré called Štìpán. Will held it by the shoulder pads, moved to her side, and put the coat on her.

He lowered his head.

"What happened in there?" she asked.

Will looked up, but didn't answer. His greenish blue eyes were bloodshot but nevertheless shinning and alert. He was, she decided, a handsome man.

She lit a cigarette and stuck it in the corner of her mouth. "I'll recommend that you get a commendation." Her cell phone rang. The number was withheld, though she knew it was the Agency calling because only it had this number. As she raised it to her ear, she thought she saw the tiniest smile on Will's face.

A man spoke to her with a deep, strident, voice. He didn't introduce himself, although Ellie knew exactly who he was: Charles Sheridan, a senior CIA officer who'd proven throughout his career in espionage that he was in equal measure very capable, ruthless, and, in Ellie's opinion, a complete dick. He told her that it annoyed the fuck out of him that the duty officer had needed to call him in on his day off because it sounded like a Category 1 protocol was about to be breached by one of their own. He asked what had happened. She told him while looking at Will. Sheridan went silent for five seconds before muttering in a more deliberate tone that Cochrane *had* been in breach of the protocol and had disobeyed orders to withdraw, that she was to tell him that his Agency exfiltration route out of Norway was now going to be shut down and that the most important men on both sides of the pond were in complete agreement that Cochrane was to surrender himself to either the British or American embassy in Oslo. Sheridan said he'd send a team to the area to try to clean up the mess, though he couldn't guarantee they'd reach the location before Norwegian cops arrived on the scene, so either way Ellie was to get out of there and return to Langley.

She closed her cell and looked at Will. "Charles Sheridan says you disobeyed orders. Why did you do it?"

"It seemed like a good idea at the time not to let them put a bullet in your brain. I'm prone to being impetuous."

He was English. She wasn't expecting that. "I thought you were SOG. Who do you work for?"

Will shrugged. "As of right now, sounds like no one." His expression became serious. "What do they want you to do with me?"

She told him what Sheridan had said.

"The embassies?" He laughed. "Nice and discreet. Tie me up, put me in a box, fly me back to the good old U.S. of A., rendered as a traitor who'll face the gallows."

"You did nothing wrong."

"You just worry about yourself now."

"You'll go to Oslo?"

"Nah, never liked the city. Beer's too expensive."

Ellie blew out smoke and tapped ash onto the ground. "Then I'll have to bring you in myself."

Will didn't respond.

"Disarm you. Put a gun to your head. Walk you out of

here." Ellie's expression was focused as she kept her eyes on him. "Trouble is, that's not an easy option."

Will held her gaze. "I'm not in the business of hurting female colleagues."

With sarcasm in her voice, Ellie said, "How very chivalrous of you." She dropped her cigarette onto the ground and extinguished it with her foot. "No. The option's not easy because . . ." She left her sentence incomplete as she nodded toward the bodies of the men Will had killed to save her life.

Will momentarily followed her gaze. "I just did my job."

"Yeah. *Your* job. Not an Agency job. At least, not after it told you to back down."

"Perhaps I should have backed down."

A large part of Ellie wanted to disagree and tell him that nobody had ever put their neck on the line to save her in the way that Will had done today. But she was still attempting to get the measure of Will, and responded, "Perhaps you should have." She folded her arms and repeated, "Who do you work for?"

"I'm a joint MI6-CIA officer."

"Joint?" Ellie frowned. "Paramilitary? Freelance?"

"No. Full-time intelligence officer."

Ellie's mind raced. Though the Agency and MI6 frequently ran joint missions and shared freelance assets, she'd never heard of an individual being used as a full-time employee of both organizations. The man before her had to be highly unusual. "I think you're in a classified task force."

Will was silent.

"Not one run by Sheridan. But maybe one that he'd dearly like to shut down because he wasn't given the glory of running the force."

Will said nothing.

"And today you gifted him that opportunity by disobeying orders. But it goes beyond that, doesn't it? Because those orders have to relate to some serious shit. What's this about?"

Will nodded toward the cabin where Ellie had met Herald. "I could ask you the same thing. What happened in there?"

Ever the consummate actor, Ellie shrugged and lied in a totally convincing way, "It's as we suspected: Herald was under suspicion by the Russians. They came here to permanently shut his mouth."

"I don't believe you're telling me everything."

Though she didn't show it, Will's perception caught Ellie by surprise. "Why not?"

"Because you're standing here talking to me, when instead you should be getting as far away from here as possible before cops show up."

"Maybe I just want to spend a few moments with the man who saved my life."

"Touching, but impractical. I doubt a deep-cover officer like you wants to get anywhere near a Norwegian police cell."

"Jail doesn't scare me."

"No. But having your cover blown does." Will admired the great strength of character Ellie had shown by winking at him when she was faced with the likelihood of her own death. Moreover, for the first time in his life he believed he was standing before someone who, like him, truly understood what it was like to operate in the very darkest recesses of the secret world. Plus, he liked her on sight. But, he knew that he had to be mentally one step ahead of her.

Ellie felt the same way about Will.

Will continued, "You're standing here because you want to know why the Agency was prepared to let you die."

"Obviously."

"Less obvious is the possibility that you're in possession of information that's unsettled you. Information that maybe you want to share with me, if you decide to trust me. Herald information."

Ellie held her fingertips together against her mouth and studied Will. Should she tell him what Herald had said before the Russian team stormed the cabin? Say nothing and walk away without knowing why the Agency had been willing to sacrifice her? Leave Will to the dogs? Help him? It all came down to a matter of trust.

Trouble was, trust was a dangerous concept in her line of work.

Will knew what she was thinking. "It's a judgment call."

"It is indeed. And what's your judgment of me?"

"My judgment's incomplete and therefore flawed. But we're running out of time. Maybe you have something for me and I have something for you. And maybe they're linked. We have to make a decision."

Every instinct told Ellie to keep her mouth shut and walk away. She'd survived her entire deep-cover career by making it a rule to never put her faith in others in the field. Today should be no exception.

But it was.

The CIA had been willing to have her killed. Herald had told her that there was a Russian mole at the top of the Agency. And she was standing before a man who'd not only risked his life to save hers, but was also paying a huge price for doing so.

She was silent for one minute before making a decision. "Herald told me the Agency is compromised. A Russian mole's sitting in Agency senior management."

Will's eyes narrowed. "Identity? Other details?"

"Nothing else, aside from Herald telling me to trust no one. We were then snatched before he could tell me more."

Will shook his head and muttered to himself, "Shit, shit."

"Does it mean anything to you?"

"On face value, nothing. But I'm trying to put the pieces together of what happened here today, and maybe that will help me understand more about the mole. Have you heard of Project Ferryman?"

Ellie shook her head.

"It's what nearly got you killed and why Langley wants to cut off my balls. It's a CIA operation, by all accounts highly classified. I reckon even the duty officer who told me to back off wasn't cleared to know about its relevance to what happened here. But I'm also betting your man Sheridan *is* Ferryman cleared, considering he was called in." He pointed toward one of the mountains. "Earlier, a senior Russian spy sat there, watching over everything. The men who attacked you were doing so under his orders. His code name's Antaeus. I had him in my sights and should have been allowed to kill the bastard. Ferryman protocols blocked me from doing so." He shook his head. "Antaeus will be long gone by now."

"Do you know what Project Ferryman is?"

"No. But here's the thing . . ."

Ellie interjected, "Top Russian spy turns up in person here to oversee the execution of Herald; Herald knows there's a high-ranking Russian mole in the Agency; you're told to back down because of an Agency operation called Project Ferryman. Ergo . . ."

"Ergo there's a link between them all, and as a result I'm fucked, the Agency's fucked, and"—Will smiled—"you came very close to a fate worse than being fucked."

Ellie laughed. "Quite." Her expression changed. "I could take this to the FBI."

"You could."

"But Sheridan told me our countries' leaders personally authorized your incarceration for breaching protocols. That means . . ."

"They've bought into the significance of Ferryman and you could be in danger of compromising Western security if you go to the feds and try to blow this open."

Ellie walked to Herald, crouched beside his dead body, placed his hand in hers, and whispered, "Thanks for the coat." She looked at Will. "Herald could be a pain in the ass, always waffling on about crap, loving the sound of his voice. But I liked him. He gave me invaluable insight into Russian secrets. And he put his life on the line for me."

"As you did for him."

"Yeah, as we all do. And on and on it goes until we all fall down." She gently rested Herald's hand on his chest, stood, and asked, "What are you going to do?"

"I'm not sure I should tell you."

Ellie shrugged. "Why not? We've done the foreplay, moved to second base, might as well go the whole distance."

Will faced west toward the mountains. "I'm going to try to get to the States and find out what Ferryman is."

Ellie moved to his side. "You think you can make it that far? European agencies will be put on your trail."

"I've got to try."

"Even if you make it to the States, they'll shoot you before you get anywhere near Langley and the answers."

"What other choice do I have?"

"Two choices. Either give yourself up and I'll support your actions. Or disappear, get a new identity, and forget all about Ferryman."

"Is that what you'd do if you were in my situation? Surrender or vanish?"

Ellie followed his gaze toward the mountains. "Surrender? No. But vanishing's something I excel at."

"And you'd do it now if you were in my shoes?"

"I . . ." She turned to face him. "Look, I don't know what I'd do." She smiled. "But I do know that there's no more 007 days for you, Mr. Bond. You've just had your license to kill revoked. No chance of you getting access to Project Ferryman."

"I could track Sheridan down and make him talk."

"Tough-guy stuff? You could end up being put in jail for laying a hand on such a high-ranking U.S. official."

"True. It's also unworkable. For the same reason you can't go the feds, I can't confront Sheridan until I know the details of Project Ferryman. It seems Ferryman's of vital importance to our countries. I can't just blunder into the States to get answers. I could compromise something that's beyond our comprehension."

"Beyond my life, judging by what happened today."

"Exactly," Will said. "Sorry, that was insensitive. I—"

"Stop." Ellie fixed another cigarette in her mouth, lit it, and winked at him in the same way she'd done before. "You want to be insensitive, then start patronizing me."

"Fair point."

Ellie nodded. "There. Fourth base achieved—first lovers' tiff." She exhaled smoke and said in a measured and cold tone, "There is another potential option open to you."

"I know."

"You'd considered it already?"

"I'd considered it, and rejected it."

"Why?"

"Because, like you, I don't put my faith in other people."

Given that Ellie had been internally wrestling with her lack of faith in others only moments before, it made her uneasy that Will had the very same thoughts. With her back to him, she walked a few paces closer to the mountains and thrust her hands into Herald's coat pockets.

Will watched her as she stood motionless, just staring at the stunning vista. Large snowflakes began to slowly descend in the windless air.

"I've spent ten years as a deep-cover operative." Ellie's voice sounded distant. "You know what that means?"

"Yes." Will knew that it meant she'd spent five years longer than the maximum time an intelligence officer could expect to operate undercover before the constant state of paranoia and fear would finally take its toll on even the strongest mind. "Why have you stayed in the field so long?"

"Because I was never interested in a desk job in Langley."

"Is that your only reason?"

Ellie hesitated before answering, "Thought I was doing some good."

"For the States?"

"For the people who live there, yeah."

"The Agency should have pulled you out of the field. You're on borrowed time. I'm surprised you're not dead in a ditch somewhere with a bullet in the back of your head."

"Thanks for the mental image."

"It's one you've thought of every day during the last ten years."

"It is." She turned to face him. "And you know what I've concluded about that image?"

"You've accepted it, and that's how you survived so long in the field."

She nodded. "But the thing is—"

"You never thought you could be shot with the blessing of the Agency."

"Nor needing to be rescued by a guy who's on the run." She pulled out another cigarette, stared at it, and replaced it in the pack. "You saved my life. That matters. But what also matters to me is that I've gone above and beyond what the Agency should have expected from me, and in return they've stuck the knife in me. So, I can no longer put my faith in the organization. And that means I'm faced with the choice of putting my faith in nothing or something."

"Something?"

"You." She folded her arms. "The only option that makes sense."

That option was for Ellie to return to Langley, pretend to senior management that she'd tried to persuade Will to surrender to the embassies in Oslo, somehow gain access to the Project Ferryman files, and relay what she'd discovered to Will if he made it to the States.

"If you get caught they'll—"

"Oh, come on!" Ellie made no attempt to hide the sarcasm in her voice. "Don't give me a pep talk about risk, okay? I know this stuff backward. Just don't."

Will made a decision. "Okay. Get a pay-as-you-go cell phone. Not in your name. Deposit its number at a DLB in Washington, D.C." He gave her the precise location of the dead-letter box. "If it rings, it'll only be me. But you might not hear from me for a while. No idea how long it's going to take to get to America. Given you're a deep-cover operative, I'm assuming you know how to get stuff? In particular, disguises and people's home addresses."

Ellie nodded.

"Okay. I'll need a lockup or an apartment in D.C. Someplace on the outskirts and cheap. And I'll need you to procure and store some things for me there." He told her what he had in mind, and drew out his wad of cash to give her money.

But Ellie walked up to him and said, "You'll need every cent you've got. I'll get you what you want. We can settle up later."

Will held out his hand.

Ellie shook his hand and held it for a few seconds, staring at the scars on his fingers. It surprised her that holding his warm hand made her feel so good. "We need to go."

"We do." Will looked at the place where earlier he'd had Russia's best spymaster in his sights. "Antaeus was here in person to make sure we didn't learn about his mole." He fixed his gaze on Ellie. "Be *very* careful. Trust no one."

FOUR

EIGHTEEN HOURS LATER, Alistair entered a large board-room in the CIA headquarters in Langley. The MI6 controller, co-head of the joint CIA-MI6 task force, had been summoned here because he was Will Cochrane's boss. The other co-head, CIA officer Patrick, was already in the room, sitting on a chair facing three people on the other side of a large oak table. The room was nothing like the others in the sprawling headquarters: it had oak paneling on the walls, leather-upholstered chairs, and ornate oil lamps that emitted a flickering bronze glow through their tulip-shaped glass bulbs; on the table was a tea set and doilies that would have looked at home in Claridge's hotel. Alistair had been in this room twice before, once to talk in fluent Arabic to a visiting Arab prince who was young and charming and naive to the nastier ways of the world, and latterly to advise the head of the Agency that MI6 was certain the Chinese had recruited an employee of the NSA.

On each occasion he'd been here, the room reminded him of the officers' quarters on a seventeenth-century man-of-war ship.

The slim, middle-aged controller was, as ever, immaculately dressed, wearing a blue three-piece suit, a French-cuff silk shirt with a cutaway collar, a tie that had been bound in a Windsor knot, and black Church's shoes. His blond hair was trimmed and lacquered in the style of an Edwardian gentleman.

Patrick looked similar to Alistair and was the same age. But today, the CIA officer had not opted to match Alistair's immaculate look; he wasn't wearing a jacket or tie, and his shirtsleeves were rolled up to reveal his sinewy and scarred forearms. Alistair knew from experience that his informal attire meant the CIA officer had contempt for the men opposite him and was pissed off.

Alistair sat next to him and studied the three people on the other side of the table. Though he knew of them, he'd never met them in person before. The man directly opposite him was Colby Jellicoe, a former high-ranking CIA officer and now an influential senator who sat on the Senate Select Committee on Intelligence, an oversight body that was tasked with ensuring that the CIA operated within the rule of law. Next to him were CIA director Ed Parker and senior CIA officer Charles Sheridan.

Jellicoe spoke first. "The Norwegians got there before we could, and they're saying there are dead American spies on their turf and they want to know why."

Alistair placed the tips of his fingers together. "Dead Americans? Oh dear."

"Yeah, well, they've been made to look like Americans, anyways." The senator picked up a pen and jabbed it in the direction of Alistair. "We're now at the diplomatic shit storm stage of a cluster fuck."

"What a delightful turn of phrase." Alistair was analyzing Jellicoe. Probably mid-fifties, short, fat—no, fat in places, wrists were normal size, face was jowly rather than round, probably he'd lost and gained weight throughout his life, but he wasn't naturally fat. What did that mean? He was a binger, yes, a man who at times couldn't resist being a gourmand, a pig. That was decided then: Jellicoe was a pig. "I'm sure you can placate the Norwegian government with a little honesty and perhaps a reminder about the nature of false-flag operations."

Jellicoe looked over the top of his glasses with an expression of utter hostility. "That's providing we want to try and placate anyone."

"Try *to*."

"What?"

"Try *to*. Never mind." Alistair smiled. "Let me guess—you'd like to use this . . . cluster fuck to enable your own agenda."

"And what might that agenda be?"

"There are many possibilities, but I've not yet settled on one. But don't worry, it'll come to me. All I need you to do is to keep opening your mouth."

Jellicoe leaned back in his chair, huffed, and tossed his pen onto the table.

Ed Parker picked up the reins. "You can't protect Cochrane."

Alistair nodded. "Of course we can't, because we don't know where he is."

"You got a number where we can call him?"

Alistair answered truthfully. "No. We had to have him completely off the radar in Norway."

"Has he called you?"

"No."

"Likely to?"

"I sincerely doubt he would."

"Why not?"

"Because he'll assume my phone is being monitored by people like you."

"Doesn't matter. We will inevitably get him."

"Inevitably?" What did Alistair think of Parker? Honest face, no anger or hostility in his voice, instead his tone was quiet and resigned, and a moment ago he'd made the briefest of glances at Jellicoe with an expression that said he was uncomfortable with what the senator was saying, or with the situation, or with Jellicoe himself. Alistair decided it was all of those things. But Parker was here because he followed orders. Despite being one of the eight directors who reported to the Director of the CIA, and despite his good nature, he was a weak bureaucrat, a plodder. "Patrick and I have direct lines to our respective premiers, men who've always been very keen to ensure that Mr. Cochrane's free to do his work. Because we've no means of getting hold of Cochrane, you'd be doing us a courtesy by *inevitably* capturing him. But that's where it will end. We'll whisk him away and put him back in the field."

"No you won't." This came from Charles Sheridan.

"And why not?"

"We'll come to that."

"Oh good, because I do like suspense." His eyes took in everything he could see of Sheridan. Tall man, early forties, a full head of brown hair that was short at the sides and back, probably meant he was ex-military, the type who thinks that all civilians need a few toughen-you-up years of national service so that the world can be a more disciplined and simpler place. Though they were physically entirely different, his expression matched the hostility of Jellicoe's, and so far he'd not looked once at the senator; instead his eyes were fixed on the men before him. Sheridan completely agreed with everything Jelli-coe represented in this room. He was his ally. No, that was an overly generous assessment. There was no doubt that Jellicoe was running the show, and that meant Sheri-dan was his pawn.

Pig. Plodder. Pawn.

Alistair wondered which of the three men would speak next.

It was the pig. "We need to know more about the task force you guys run."

Patrick exclaimed, "No fucking way!"

Alistair glanced at his colleague. Oh dear God. His face was flushed, his eyes wide, and the sinews in his neck were jutting out like knife blades. When Patrick went like this, it usually meant he wanted to rip someone's head off and eat it. "What my friend means is that in order for us to comply with your request, we'd need written clearance to do so and from the highest authority."

"And that authority ain't going to give you clearance, Jellicoe!" Patrick was leaning forward.

Alistair patted a hand on Patrick's leg, knowing it would only further fuel his colleague's anger—anger that was useful in situations like this. "Gentlemen, let's sort this out amicably. I've had a rather long and turbulent flight to get here to understand why you're on the warpath because my officer wanted to kill enemy number one when he had him in his sights, and because in killing Antaeus's men he breached Project Ferryman protocols. What is Ferryman?"

Jellicoe and Sheridan laughed, and Parker averted his gaze.

"Written authorizations or otherwise, you can't expect us to tell you anything about our task force and the nature of Cochrane's work if we don't understand the implications of his actions in Norway. What is Ferryman?"

The senator composed himself. "I'll tell you exactly what Project Ferryman is. It's something much more important than your shitty little *special relationship* task force, or your loose-cannon lone wolf for that matter."

Patrick leaned back. "Thankfully, the president and British prime minister don't share that view."

Jellicoe seemed unflustered by the comment. "You think so?" He loosened the knot of his tie, undid the top button of his shirt, and rubbed his flabby throat. "Task Force S, formerly known as the Spartan Section, has been in existence for eight years, ever since Will Cochrane passed the Spartan Program." He pointed at Patrick.

"Two years ago, Cochrane landed in your lap and needed your help. You and some of your Agency colleagues started working with the Section and as a result of that work a decision was made from on high to make the unit a British-American collaboration." Jellicoe picked up his pen and started twirling around his fingers. "I can give you a blow-by-blow account of the three joint task force missions you've conducted if you like? Actually, make that four missions, if you include Cochrane's unsuccessful hunt for Cobalt."

The menace in Patrick's voice was unmistakable as he asked, "How do you know that information?"

For the first time since arriving in Langley, Alistair felt angry. "I too want to know the answer to that, before making a decision on whether to report you to my superiors for obtaining highly classified information without clearance to do so."

"Clearance?" Jellicoe withdrew a sheet of paper from his jacket, unfolded it, and placed it in the center of the table. "Your superiors?" He tapped the sheet. "You mean these guys?" He pushed the paper toward Alistair with one finger. "Take a moment to read that. Might put things in perspective."

Alistair read the brief note, recognized the two signatures at the bottom, momentarily closed his eyes while feeling utter dismay, and handed the letter to Patrick.

"This can't be possible." The Task Force S co-head's voice was trembling with rage and shock. He slammed the note onto the table and sat in stunned silence.

As did Alistair. The president and prime minister had

personally signed a letter stating that Project Ferryman had nearly been jeopardized by the actions of Will Cochrane and Task Force S, that an international warrant for Cochrane's arrest had been issued and would remain in force until Cochrane was caught and dealt with away from public scrutiny, that Alistair and Patrick were to give full assistance to Senator Colby Jellicoe in his efforts to apprehend Cochrane, and that with immediate effect Task Force S was permanently shut down.

Jellicoe grinned. "You're lucky Ferryman's still intact, or you would have been strung up rather than disbanded. Try and"—his smile broadened—"try to understand that Cochrane's a dead man walking, and his bosses have just had their balls cut off."

FIVE

EVEN THOUGH THE sun had started rising only minutes earlier, the occupants of the Norwegian coastal home were clearly awake, with smoke billowing from one of its chimneys and interior lights switched on. It had two small outbuildings and a barn, and in front of them a small trawler boat was moored alongside a jetty on a thin inlet of the sea. The place was in a flat valley, carpeted in snow and an icy early-morning mist, and was surrounded by hills. Will was on one of the hills, staring at the isolated encampment. He'd walked forty-two miles north to reach the location.

Shivering violently, he watched the place for four hours, saw an older man and three younger men coming and going from buildings, and a woman and a teenage girl doing chores. Will's physical situation was bad. He'd had no food for two days, and his weak state meant his body was struggling to generate heat.

By midday the sun was up high in the cloudless sky but the temperature was still dreadfully cold, at least fifteen degrees below freezing. Will saw the men get into a pickup truck and drive off the property along its only track. When they were gone, Will rose to his feet, brushed snow and ice from his face, and shuffled painfully down an escarpment until he was in the valley. Keeping the outhouses between him and the main residence, he carefully moved forward, desperate not to be seen by the woman or the girl. He reached the jetty, moved along it in a crouch until he was beside the trawler, and searched the boat's metal hull. He found what he was looking for, close to the bow on the vessel's port side. Crouching lower, he looked at the fist-sized circle that had been scratched on the hull's paint. He took out his handgun, ejected the magazine, and used the gun clip to scratch a cross within the circle. Replacing the magazine in the gun, he carefully made his way back off the jetty, past the outbuildings, and back up the escarpment.

Three hours later the vehicle and men returned. Will's teeth and jaw were shuddering uncontrollably, but he didn't care because nobody could hear him here. The men exited their truck and went about their duties.

After a further two hours it was dark. Will was lying on his front, his arms wrapped around his chest even though they did nothing to get him warm. His breathing was shallow and he could taste blood in his mouth; his eyeballs throbbed in agony from the cold; the shaking continued. The house was fully illuminated again, with two exterior lights switched on as well as tiny lights lining

the jetty. Will imagined that the occupants of the settle-
ment were sitting down in their house to a hot dinner and
drinks. He desperately wanted to go down there, to find
any shelter and warmth, but he knew he had to wait.

Seven hours later, it was midnight. Only one light was
illuminated within the house, but the outside lights were
still switched on. The older man stepped out of the house's
sea-facing door, stopped, lit a cigarette or cigar, and blew
smoke before walking along the jetty. He moved to the
front of the pier, turned toward the trawler, crouched
down for a brief moment, stood again, walked back to
the house, and disappeared inside. Will hauled himself to
his feet, staggered, collapsed onto his knees, raised himself up again, and took agonizing steps down the hill and
into the valley. His mind was a daze and he barely knew
if things around him were real anymore. He desperately
tried to stay conscious but felt that he was minutes away
from losing the last remaining mental strength he had.
Using a hand against the walls of the outbuildings to
steady himself, he staggered to the jetty. He collapsed
to the snow-covered ground, silently cursed, knew that
he could no longer stand, and instead used his hands to
pull himself inch by inch along the jetty. Snow entered
his mouth; he tried to spit it out, gave up trying to do so,
but kept pulling himself along the walkway until he was
by the trawler's bow. He looked at the circle and cross
scratched on the hull.

Three horizontal lines had been engraved over both.

It was the covert signal telling him that the Norwegian captain of this trawler knew the British intelligence

officer was nearby, that it was safe for him to approach the house, and that the captain was ready to sail him out of this country.

Will rolled onto his back and stared at the spectacular star-filled sky before his eyes closed without him wishing them to do so. He wondered how long it would be before the captain found his frozen dead body.

SIX

FBI DIRECTOR Bo Haupman had long ago decided that the CIA was a rootless entity because it wasn't law enforcement, military, or civilian. Its officers reflected that amorphous state; they were soulless creatures who, when asked to explain what results they'd achieved and how those results mattered one bit to the man on the street, would look coy and use the excuse of secrecy to avoid the question, when in reality they just plain and simple didn't have a concrete answer. For sure, post-9/11 the Agency had taken the lead on counterterrorism work, turning many of its young bucks into John Wayne wannabes who relished the prospect of swapping their suits and attaché cases and diplomatic life for a dishdasha, an AK-47, and a tent on an Afghan mountainside. Right now, they had a bit of tangible purpose—we shot this bad guy, did a predator drone strike against this bunch of crazies, put this leader into a cell with only a blanket and a bucket of water and three burly men for company. But you could see in their eyes that they knew the party wouldn't last forever, that pretty soon they'd be going back to the world of paper reports, cocktails, agonizingly boring analysis, and the only highlight of their lives being the opportunity to listen in on a telephone intercept and learn that a terrorist's wife wants her husband to pick up some potatoes, chicken, and cabbage for dinner.

That's not to say he disliked all Agency officers. Put them in a room with a drink in their hands and they could be great company, because they'd go out of their way to talk about anything other than their work. Put a bunch of feds in a room and within five minutes all of them would be talking about how the perps are getting away with murder because the Bureau's snowed under with paperwork. Yes, Agency people could be light relief.

Charles Sheridan wasn't.

On more than one occasion, Bo had gotten himself to sleep by fantasizing about clubbing the high-ranking CIA officer to death and dumping his body in the middle of a lake.

Not that Bo could actually do that. Despite having shot a few scum in his career, and being the size of a bear that was a few years past its prime, Bo was a gentle man, and it had come as a relief when promotion had enabled him to swap his sidearm for a desk.

Still, the fantasy remained, and he imagined doing it to Sheridan right now as the CIA officer placed his leather bag on the floor, removed a raincoat that matched the style Agency and Secret Service characters wore in the movies, slumped into a chair, and gave Bo his sternest Chairman of the Joint Chiefs of Staff look. A look that was undeserved, given that Sheridan had retired from the infantry with the rank of major before joining the Agency.

They were in a small room in the Bureau's headquarters in the J. Edgar Hoover building. Bo had chosen the room as it had no table in it, and was informal and unimpressive. That would grate on Sheridan, because he would have expected the red-carpet treatment for someone of his seniority and power.

Bo gestured toward the woman next to him and asked Sheridan, "You don't mind if my secretary takes notes, do you?"

"I'd rather she didn't."

"I only asked out of courtesy."

"Do what you want, then."

"And what do *you* want?"

Sheridan glanced at the secretary. "You sure she should be in the room?"

Bo smiled, hoping he looked condescending. "The last time you and I spoke without notes being taken, you reported the content of our conversation to the head of the Agency. I didn't mind, though I was concerned when I heard that your interpretation of what was said was . . . less than truthful." Bo placed his ankle on his other leg. "In any case, she's security cleared."

"Not by us."

Bo waved a hand dismissively. "But she is by me, so she stays. What do you want?"

Sheridan stared at the secretary for a few seconds before locking his gaze back on Bo. "I want a bloodhound."

"A Bureau bloodhound?"

"No, a frickin' NYPD bloodhound," he huffed, causing small flecks of spit to stick to his lips. "Of course a Bureau bloodhound. Otherwise I wouldn't be wasting my time in this shitty place."

"Would you like a cup of coffee?"

"No."

"Tea?"

"No."

"Water?"

"No."

"Anything else that might put you at ease?"

"I am at . . ." Sheridan looked irritated as he scratched fingers against his hair and examined his nails. "Look, let's just get this over with. I need your best officer."

"To do a manhunt."

"That's what I said on the phone."

"On U.S. soil?"

"I doubt it."

"Then why don't you guys take up the challenge?"

"Because this is a matter that's being overseen by the Senate committee, and the SSCI doesn't like it when the Agency plays cops."

"Of course, plus there's the small matter that you're not very good at it." Bo continued to imagine swinging his baseball bat at Sheridan's head. "Who is he?"

Sheridan pointed at the secretary. "Tell her to stop writing!"

"I will do no such . . ."

Sheridan leaned toward the secretary. "You can listen to your boss, lady, or you can listen to me. Keep taking notes, and I'll ensure you're put in prison for threatening national security."

The secretary darted a look at Bo, raising her eyebrows.

Bo held up his hand. "It's okay, Marsha. Let's leave the notes until Mr. Sheridan is feeling a bit more . . ." He looked directly at the CIA officer. " . . . calm."

Sheridan leaned back. "His name's Will Cochrane. British Intelligence, but he's joint with us. Last seen in Norway two days ago."

"What's he done?"

"Compromised an Agency operation. That's all you need to know and"—Sheridan raised his voice before Bo could interject—"that's all you will *ever* know."

"Have the Brits given you authority to apprehend him?"

Sheridan nodded. "You'll get the green-light paperwork and the signatories to the task. But I'm here because before I draw up those papers, I need to know if you've got an officer who's up for the job."

"A bloodhound."

"A man who hasn't failed before."

Bo was deep in thought. "Would Cochrane kill my officer to evade capture?"

Sheridan seemed to consider the question. "I think

he'd prefer another way out." He shrugged. "But if he's backed into a corner, then who knows."

"His capabilities?"

Sheridan glanced again at the secretary to ensure that she was continuing to obey his instructions. "Three years ago, he covertly entered an African war zone, shot dead the deposed dictator while he was on the run, made it look as though rebels had killed the man, and exited the country without anyone but a handful of MI6 officers knowing he was there. It was the easiest job he'd done in eight years of service."

Bo frowned. "That dictator had to be . . ."

Sheridan pointed at him. "Exactly who you're thinking of, but you keep your mouth shut about that or you'll be in a cell next door to pretty missy here."

Bo ignored the threat. "What resources does Cochrane have in Europe?"

"He's got ten thousand dollars of cash on him. Plus an alias passport and credit card, but he'll be flagged the moment he uses either."

"Then he'll stand no chance of evading capture."

Sheridan laughed. "You got much experience of hunting black-ops guys?"

Bo rolled his eyes. "You're not going to get all melodramatic on me now, are you, Charles?"

Sheridan looked unsettled; clearly he had been warming up to a bit of melodrama. "Well, either way, you don't know shit, so I'll tell it to you straight. Typically, deniable operators have three preplanned options to escape a country. The first is pretty standard: they enter a country with a false passport, they leave the same way. Providing the wheel's not fallen off, it's as straightforward as that. But if something goes wrong and we think the officer's blown, the Agency will always have in place a covert exfiltration route—cross-border, sea, air, assets in situ to help him."

"Presumably that's no longer an option for Cochrane."

"No." Sheridan grinned. "We fucked him on that one."

"So that leaves . . . ?"

Sheridan's grin vanished. "That leaves the it-annoys-the-hell-out-of-me option. See, black-ops guys and girls are a bunch of paranoids. Everyone's out to get them. Trouble is, sometimes they're not wrong."

"They put in place backup contingencies?"

"Yeah."

"Without telling the Agency?"

Sheridan nodded.

"Because it might be the Agency that's trying to . . . fuck them?"

Sheridan was motionless. "Cochrane will have at least one or two assets in Norway that we don't know about. They'll try to help him get out of the country."

"Where will he go?"

"East or south, but most certainly not west."

"Yes, I can see that west wouldn't be a particularly desirable option. You know that if you'd approached me two weeks ago, I'd have told you straight that we didn't have the resources to do another manhunt. Know why?"

"Sure. Every fed under your control was already tasked on a manhunt. Trying to find Mr. Cobalt."

Bo frowned. "Last intel we had on him was that he was moving major capital between Turkmenistan and Algeria. I still don't get why we, and every agency we know outside the States, were told to shut down that operation." His frown vanished. "You know anything about that?"

Sheridan grinned. "Not much I don't know."

"So why . . ."

"We'll get Cobalt, rest assured, but not the way we've been going about it so far. That's all I'm saying." Sheridan checked his watch. "You going to capture Cochrane, or not?"

Part of Bo wanted to tell Sheridan to give the job to another agency, because any enemy of Sheridan's couldn't be all that bad. No. That's exactly what Sheridan wanted to hear so that he could go back to the SSCI, tell them a bunch of crap, and try to persuade them that the Agency should be given the task. "Okay, we'll do it."

Sheridan looked momentarily annoyed before composing himself and giving his most insincere grin. "Great to hear, but you should know that I've been given authority to sit in your bloodhound's team and watch progress. Officially, the term is 'adviser.' But better for you to think of it as 'pain in the ass.'"

Bo had expected this. "It's an FBI operation, meaning we have primacy up to the point when we capture him. After that, you can do what you want with Cochrane. Do you know what primacy means?"

Sheridan didn't answer.

"It means that you're not an adviser or a pain in the ass. It means that for the duration of the manhunt, you're my bloodhound's *employee*."

Sheridan didn't like that description one bit. "Well, you better get your man in here, so I can meet my new *boss*."

In Bo Haupman's fantasy, he stopped beating Sheridan around the head. This was turning out to be much more fun. "When you called me to say that you needed to speak to me in person about a potential manhunt request, I thought I'd alert my best officer that you were coming."

"Good, get him in here!"

Calmly, Bo replied, "Oh, there's no need." He pointed at Marsha Gage. "My best bloodhound's been in the room with us the whole time."

About the Author

As an MI6 field officer, **MATTHEW DUNN** acted in deep-cover roles throughout the world. He was trained in all aspects of intelligence collection, deep-cover deployments, military unarmed combat, surveillance, and infiltration. During his time in MI6, Dunn conducted approximately seventy missions—all of them successful. He is the author of *Spycatcher, Sentinel, Slingshot,* and the forthcoming *Dark Spies,* all featuring Will Cochrane. He lives in England.

www.matthewdunnbooks.com

www.Facebook.com/pages/
Matthew-Dunn/168465723306908

Visit www.AuthorTracker.com for exclusive information on your favorite HarperCollins authors.